The ladder wobbled; *she* wobbled.

Mason instinctively reached up to steady her.

But as his hands caught her around the waist, his palms came into contact with the smooth warm skin of her exposed midriff.

He heard her inhale sharply, saw her eyes widen and felt the air crackle around them.

The moment seemed to spin out between them, reflected in the emotions that swirled through the depths of her dark eyes.

Surprise.

Confusion.

Awareness.

Desire.

Apparently the needs that were churning inside of him were churning inside of her, too.

And wasn't that a lucky coincidence?

Dear Reader,

At some point in our lives, each one of us has been, or will be, affected by breast cancer—if not directly, then through the diagnosis of a family member or friend.

The number of cases that are identified every year is staggering. The good news is that advances in detection and treatment have allowed more women not just to survive but to resume healthy and active lives.

Zoe is a fictional character whose creation was inspired by the stories of real women who have faced cancer and had the strength and courage to talk about it. Her story is that of a woman rediscovering the joys of living and loving.

I hope you enjoy sharing her journey.

Best,

Brenda Harlen

P.S. I will be donating a portion of my royalties from the sale of this book to breast cancer research.

THE NEW GIRL
IN TOWN

BRENDA HARLEN

SPECIAL EDITION®

Published by Silhouette Books

America's Publisher of Contemporary Romance

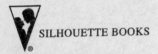

SILHOUETTE BOOKS

ISBN-13: 978-0-373-24859-9
ISBN-10:   0-373-24859-8

THE NEW GIRL IN TOWN

Copyright © 2007 by Brenda Harlen

Visit Silhouette Books at www.eHarlequin.com

Printed in U.S.A.

BRENDA HARLEN

grew up in a small town surrounded by books and imaginary friends. Although she always dreamed of being a writer, she chose to follow a more traditional career path first. After two years of practicing as an attorney, including an appearance in front of the Supreme Court of Canada, she gave up her "real" job to be a mom and to try her hand at writing books. Three years, five manuscripts and another baby later, she sold her first book—an RWA Golden Heart Winner—to Silhouette Books.

Brenda lives in southern Ontario with her real-life husband/hero, two heroes-in-training and two neurotic dogs. She is still surrounded by books ("too many books," according to her children) and imaginary friends, but she also enjoys communicating with real people. Readers can contact Brenda by e-mail at brendaharlen@yahoo.com or by snail mail c/o Silhouette Books, 233 Broadway, Suite 1001, New York, NY 10279.

This book is dedicated to everyone
who has fought the fight against breast cancer with
courage and strength—you are an inspiration.
And to the memory of those who ultimately
lost the battle—you are not forgotten.

With thanks to the researchers,
doctors and other health-care professionals
who offer direction and hope.

Chapter One

Zoe Kozlowski definitely wasn't in Manhattan anymore.

Years of living in the city had acclimated her to the sounds of traffic—the squeal of tires, the blare of horns, the scream of sirens. She would no doubt have slept through the pounding of a jackhammer six stories below her open bedroom window or the wail of a fire truck speeding past her apartment building, but the gentle trilling of sparrows shattered the cocoon of her slumber.

In time, she was certain she would get used to these sounds, too, but for now, they were new and enchanting enough that she didn't mind being awakened at such an early hour. As she carried her cup of decaf chai tea out onto the back porch, she could hear not just the birds but the gentle breeze rustling the leaves and, in the distance, the barking of a dog.

She stepped over a broken board and settled onto the top step to survey her surroundings in the morning light. The colors were so vivid and bright it almost hurt to look at them—the brilliantly polished sapphire of the sky broken only by the occasional fluffy white cloud. And the trees—there were so many kinds, so many shades of green around the perimeter of the yard. Evergreens whose sweeping branches ranged in hue from deep emerald to silvery sage. Oaks and maples and poplars with leaves of various shapes and sizes and colors of yellow-green and dark green and every tone in between.

She found herself wondering how it would look in the fall—what glorious shades of gold and orange and rust and red would appear. And then in the winter, when the leaves had fallen to the ground and the trees were bare, the long branches glistening with frost or dusted with snow. And in the early spring, when the first buds began to unfurl and herald the arrival of the new season.

But now, edging toward the first days of summer, everything was green and fresh and beautiful. And while she appreciated the natural beauty of the present, she was already anticipating the changing of the seasons. Not wishing her life away, but looking to her future here and planning to enjoy every minute of it.

She knew the yard was in as serious need of work as the old house in which she'd spent the night, but as she took another look around, she was filled with a deep sense of peace and satisfaction that everything she saw was hers.

She'd get a porch swing, she decided suddenly, impulsively. Where she could sit to enjoy her first cup of tea every morning. She would put down roots here, just like those trees, dig deep into the soil and make this place her home.

It was strange that she'd lived in New York for almost ten years and never felt the same compelling need to put down roots there. Or maybe it just hadn't occurred to her to do so in a city made up of mostly concrete and steel. Not that she hadn't loved Manhattan. There was an aura about the city that still appealed to her, an excitement she'd never felt anywhere else. For a young photographer, it had been *the* place to be, and when Scott had suggested moving there after they were married, she'd jumped at the opportunity. They'd started out at a tiny little studio apartment in Brooklyn Heights, moved to a one-bedroom walk-up in Soho, then, finally, only four years ago, to a classic six on Park Avenue.

She'd never imagined leaving there, never imagined wanting to be anywhere else. Until a routine doctor's appointment had turned out to be not-so-routine after all.

In the eighteen months that had passed since then, her life had taken a lot of unexpected turns. The most recent of which had brought her here, to Pinehurst, New York, to visit her friend Claire and—

Oomph!

The breath rushed out of her lungs and her mug went flying from her fingers as she was knocked onto her back by a furry beast that settled on her chest.

She would have gasped if she'd had any air left to expel. Instead, she struggled to draw in enough oxygen to scream. As she opened her mouth, a big wet tongue swept over her face.

Ugh!

She wasn't sure if the hairy creature was licking her in a harmless show of affection or sampling her before it sank its teeth in. She sputtered and tried to push it away.

A shrill whistle sounded in the distance and the dog—at least, she thought it was a dog, although it didn't look like any kind she'd ever seen before—lifted its head in response to the sound. Then the tongue was back, slobbering over her again.

"Rosie!"

The animal withdrew, just far enough to plant its substantial behind on top of her thighs, trapping them beneath its impressive weight.

Zoe eyed it warily as she pushed herself up onto her elbows, bracing herself for another attack. A movement at the edge of the woods caught her attention, and she turned her head to see a tall, broad-shouldered figure moving with long-legged strides across the yard.

She shoved at the beast again, ineffectually, and blew out a frustrated breath. "Can you get this darn thing off me?" she asked through gritted teeth.

"Sorry." The man reached down to grab the animal by its collar. Zoe's irritation was forgotten as her gaze swept over her rescuer.

His hair was dark, almost black, and cut short around a face that seemed to be chiseled out of granite. His forehead was broad, his cheekbones sharp, and his nose

had a slight bump on the bridge as if it had been broken
once or twice before. His jaw was dark with stubble, and
his eyes—she couldn't be sure of the color because his
face was in shadow, but she could tell that they were
dark—were narrowed on the beast. He wore an old
Cornell University T-shirt over a pair of jeans that
molded to the lean muscles of his long legs and a
scuffed pair of sneakers.

"Are you alright?" he asked, his voice as warm and
smooth as premium-aged whiskey.

"I'm fine. Or I will be when you get this thing
away from me."

"Rosie, off." He spoke to her attacker now, the words
accompanied by a sharp tug on the collar. The four-
legged beast immediately removed its weight from her
legs and plopped down on its butt beside the man,
tongue hanging out of its mouth as it gazed at him adoringly.

Zoe figured the beast was female. She also figured
the man was used to that kind of reaction from the
women he met. She might have been inclined to drool
herself except that a half-dozen years as a fashion photographer had immunized her against the impact of
beautiful faces. Well, mostly, anyway. Because she
couldn't deny there was something about this man's
rugged good looks she found appealing enough to
almost wish she had her camera in hand.

The unexpectedness of that urge was something she
would think about later, Zoe decided as she pulled
herself to her feet, then rubbed a hand over her face to
wipe away the dog drool. She tugged at the frayed hem

of the cut-off shorts she'd pulled on when she'd rolled out of bed, conscious of the fact that they fell only a couple of inches below the curve of her butt.

"What the heck is that thing?" she asked, taking a deliberate step back from man and beast.

"He's a dog," the man responded in the same whiskey-smooth tone. "And although he's overly affectionate at times, he doesn't usually take to strangers."

"Obviously it's a dog." At least it had four paws and wagging tail. "But what kind? I've never seen anything so—" *ugly* was the description that immediately came to mind, but she didn't want to insult the man or his best friend, so she decided upon "—big."

His smile was wry. "He's of indeterminate pedigree—part deerhound, part Old English sheepdog, with a lot of other parts mixed in."

She glanced at the handsome stranger again, saw that he was giving her the same critical study she'd given his pet. She was suddenly aware that her hair needed to be combed, her teeth needed to be brushed and her T-shirt was covered in muddy paw prints. Then his gaze lifted to hers, and she forgot everything else in the realization that his eyes were as startlingly blue as the sapphire sky overhead.

"Did you ever consider putting your dog in obedience classes?" she asked. "Preferably before it—he—knocks somebody unconscious."

"As a matter of fact, Rosie graduated top of his class. He can heel, sit, lay down, roll over and speak." He shrugged and smiled again. "He just hasn't learned to curb his enthusiasm."

"No kidding," she said dryly. Then she frowned. "Did you call *him* 'Rosie'?"

"It's short for Rosencrantz."

"Rosencrantz," Zoe echoed, wondering what kind of person would inflict such torture on a helpless animal. Not that this one was helpless, but the name still seemed cruel.

"As in Rosencrantz and Guildenstern," he told her. "From *Hamlet*."

She was admittedly surprised—and more intrigued than she wanted to be by this sexy, blue-eyed, Shakespeare-reading stranger.

"Where is Guildenstern?" she asked apprehensively.

"With my brother," the man answered. "My business partner found the two puppies abandoned by the creek in his backyard. He and his wife wanted to keep them, but they already have a cat and a baby on the way, so I got one and my brother took the other."

She noticed that he spoke of his partner having a wife but didn't mention one of his own. Not that it really mattered, of course. She had a lot of reasons for moving to Pinehurst, but looking for romance was definitely not one of them—especially when the wounds of her failed marriage had barely begun to heal.

"Well, you need to keep that thing on a leash," she said, forcing her thoughts to refocus on the conversation.

The animal in question immediately dropped to its belly and whined plaintively.

Zoe frowned. "What's wrong with him?"

"You said the *L*-word," he told her.

She looked at him blankly.

"*L-E-A-S-H.*"

"You've got to be kidding."

He shook his head. "Rosie hates being tied up."

"Well, he'll have to get used to it because I don't appreciate being attacked in my own yard by your mongrel pet."

"Your yard?" He seemed surprised by her statement. "You bought this place?"

She nodded.

"Are you rich and bored? Or just plain crazy?"

She bristled at that. "You're not the first person to question my sanity," she admitted. "But you're the first who's had the nerve to do so while standing on my property."

"I'm just…surprised," he said. "The house has been on the market a long time, and I hadn't heard anything around town recently about a potential buyer."

"The final papers were signed yesterday. This is my house, my land, my space."

"If this is your house, your land, and your space, then that would mean—"

He paused to smile, and she cursed her traitorous heart for beating faster.

"—you're my neighbor."

Mason watched as her pale cheeks flushed with color, making him think she might be attractive if she cleaned herself up. Right now, however, she was a mess. Her long blond hair was tangled around her face, her brow—above incredibly gorgeous eyes the color of dark chocolate— was creased with a scowl, and her skimpy little T-shirt was covered in mud. But he couldn't help but notice that the shirt clung to curves that looked soft and round in all the right places, and he felt the stir of arousal.

He gave himself a mental shake, acknowledging that he'd definitely been too long without a woman if the sight of this disheveled little spitfire was turning him on.

His current hiatus from dating had been a matter of choice as much as necessity, since his break-up with Erica had coincided with a flurry of big jobs that had required all of his attention and focus. Recently, however, things at the office had started to slow down a little. Enough at least that he could catch a decent amount of sleep at night and maybe even consider getting out socially again. If he did, maybe he'd meet a woman who was more his usual type.

But it was this woman who had his attention now. Because she was, if not his type, at least his neighbor, which made him naturally curious about her.

"Tell me something," he said.

"What's that?" she asked warily.

"What possessed a city girl like you to buy an abandoned old house like this?"

"What makes you think I'm a city girl?"

He allowed his gaze to move over her again, lingering, appraising. "The designer clothes and fancy watch, for starters. But mostly it's the casual self-confidence layered over restless energy that says to hell with the rest of the world and somehow fits you as perfectly as those snug little denim shorts."

She tilted her chin. "That's quite an assumption to make after a five-minute conversation."

He smiled. "I enjoy studying people—and women are a particular interest of mine."

"I don't doubt that's true," she said dryly.

He wasn't dissuaded by the comment or her tone. "You never did answer my question about why you bought this house."

"It's a beautiful house."

"It might have been a dozen years ago," he allowed. "Before Mrs. Hadfield got too old and too tight-fisted to pay for the repairs."

"What happened to Mrs. Hadfield?" she asked, in what seemed to him a blatant attempt to change the subject.

"She passed away about eighteen months ago, left the house to a grandson who lives in California. He put it on the market right away, but there was only one early offer on the property and he refused to sell to a developer, insisting his grandmother wouldn't have wanted the house torn down and the land divided."

After that deal had fallen through, Mason had learned from the real estate agent that the grandson had some specific ideas about the type of person Beatrice Hadfield wanted living in her house after she was gone. But he'd refused to elaborate on the criteria, even to the agent, and she'd mostly given up on selling the house— until now, apparently.

"And you know about this unsuccessful sale because…" she prompted.

"Because there are no secrets in a small town."

"Great," she muttered. "And I hated feeling like my neighbors were on top of me in the city."

She really wasn't his type, but she was female and kind of cute, and he couldn't resist teasing, "I'll only be on top if that's where you want me, darlin'."

Her chocolate eyes narrowed as she drew herself up to her full height—which was about a foot shorter than his six feet two inches. "It won't be," she said coolly. "And don't call me 'darling.'"

He held up his hands in mock surrender. "I didn't mean to offend you…" He paused, giving her the chance to offer her name.

"My name is Zoe," she finally told him. "Zoe Kozlowski."

It was an unusual name but pretty, and somehow it suited her. "Mason Sullivan."

She eyed his outstretched hand for a moment before shaking it.

Rosie barked and held up a paw.

His new neighbor glanced down, the hint of a smile tugging at the corners of her mouth. He found himself staring at that mouth, wondering if her lips were as soft and kissable as they looked.

Way too long without a woman.

"You didn't tell me he could shake," she said, removing her hand from his to take the paw Rosie offered.

"Another of his many talents," he said, oddly perturbed that she seemed more interested in his dog than in him. Not that *he* was interested in *her*, but he did have a reputation in town for his success with the ladies, and never before had one thrown him over for an animal.

"Now if only you could teach him to respect the boundary line between our properties."

"That might take some time," he warned, as she released Rosie's paw and straightened again. "He's become accustomed to running through these woods over the past several months."

"It won't take any time at all if you keep him tied up," she said.

Rosie whimpered as though he understood the threat, compelling Mason to protest on the animal's behalf.

"He's a free spirit," he said, then smiled. "Like me."

She tilted her head, studying him like she would a worrisome crack in a basement foundation. "Do the women in this town actually fall for such tired lines?"

It was an effort to keep the smile in place, but he wouldn't give her the satisfaction of letting it fade. "I haven't had any complaints."

"I worked at *Images* in New York City for six years," she said, citing one of the industry's leading fashion magazines. "I spent most of my days surrounded by men who made their living playing a part for the camera, so it's going to take more than a smile to make me melt."

Okay, so she was tougher than he'd expected. But he hadn't yet met a woman who was immune to his charm—it was only a matter of finding the right buttons to push. "That sounds like a challenge."

"Just a statement of fact," she told him, bending to pick up a mug that he guessed Rosie had knocked from her hand with the exuberance of his greeting. "Now if you'll excuse me, I have things to do today."

He stepped down off the porch, his hand still holding onto the dog's collar, his eyes still on his new neighbor. "It was nice meeting you, Zoe."

"It was certainly interesting," she said, but with a half smile that allowed him to hope she wasn't still annoyed at Rosie's manner of introduction.

And as he turned toward his own home, he found himself already looking forward to his next encounter with his new neighbor.

Zoe walked into the house with a smile on her face and a positive outlook for the day despite—or maybe because of—the unexpected events of the morning. Though she couldn't have anticipated meeting one of her neighbors in the backyard, and so early, she thought she'd handled the situation. She'd even managed to engage in a casual conversation without worrying too much about where he was looking or what he was thinking. It was a gloriously liberating experience.

Mason Sullivan was a stranger who knew nothing of her or her past, a dog owner simply apologizing for the affectionate nature of his pet. He was a man who'd looked at her like she was a woman—a completely normal interaction that followed a year and a half of wondering if anything would ever seem normal again.

In the past eighteen months, she'd lost everything that mattered: her husband, her job, her home, and—most devastating of all—her sense of self. She'd packed most of what she had left into a tiny storage unit, loaded a dozen boxes in the back of her car, then driven out of the city, determined to start her life over again somewhere new. What she really wanted was to go someplace where no one knew who she was, where no one would look at her with pitying glances or talk to her in sympathetic murmurs. Someplace where she could pretend she was still the woman she used to be.

What she'd found—on a visit to Claire, her best friend and confidante—was a charming Victorian house that caught her attention so completely she actually stopped her car right in the middle of the road to stare.

It was an impressive three stories of turrets and towers despite having been badly neglected and in desperate need of repair. The roof on the wraparound porch was sagging, the chimneys were crumbling, paint was peeling, and several of the windows were boarded up.

As Zoe studied the broken parts of the whole, she had to fight back tears. There was no doubt the house had once been strong and proud and beautiful. Now it was little more than a shadow of its former self—abandoned, neglected and alone.

Just as she was.

She almost didn't see the For Sale sign that was mostly hidden by the weeds that had taken over the front garden, but when she did, she knew that it was meant to be hers. She'd pulled her car off the road and into a gravel driveway as overgrown with weeds as the yard, then picked up her cell phone and dialed the number on the sign.

For the past year and a half, she'd been looking for some direction and purpose, and here, at last, she'd found it.

Or maybe she really was crazy.

She acknowledged that possibility as she set her mug in the sink. But even if she was, she was committed now. The house was hers—along with the weighty mortgage she'd secured for the purchase and improvements. And though there was a part of her that was terrified to think she'd made a huge mistake, another—bigger—part of her was excited by the challenges and opportunities that lay ahead.

She was going to fix up this broken-down house and turn it into a successful bed-and-breakfast. Although there were several such establishments already in town, none were as majestic as the building that was now her home. Or as majestic as she knew it would be when she was finished with it.

She glanced at her watch, noted that it was almost eight o'clock. The architect—who happened to be the husband of the lawyer who'd helped her purchase the property—was due to arrive in a little more than half an hour.

She was excited about meeting him, anxious to get started. But she also felt the first niggle of doubt, a twinge of uncertainty. It was one thing to spin elaborate dreams inside her mind, and something else entirely to share these hopes with someone who could help her realize them—or destroy them.

As she made her way across the dusty floor, questions and doubts dogged her every step.

What *was* she doing?

It was what her friends and colleagues had asked when she'd walked away from her job at the magazine. They'd expressed sympathy for what she'd been through but on the whole agreed that the best thing for Zoe was to maintain the status quo as much as possible. She thought it ironic—and more than a little irritating—that so many people who hadn't been through what she had could have so much advice about how to cope.

It was only Claire who really understood. And it was Claire who agreed Zoe should live the life she wanted to live rather than the one she had; Claire who knew that sometimes a person needed a new beginning in order to continue. And Claire had been thrilled when her friend had chosen Pinehurst for that fresh start. Admittedly, her excitement had been tempered by apprehension when she'd seen the house Zoe intended to buy, but her support had never wavered.

As Zoe batted away a cobweb, she wondered what her former colleagues in Manhattan would think now. Then she shook her head, refusing to let her mind continue along that path. She didn't have time for doubts or recriminations—she needed to get ready for her appointment with the architect.

The taps creaked and the pipes groaned, but Zoe managed to coax water out of the shower head in the main-floor bathroom. It wasn't very warm or clear, but it was enough to wet a washcloth to scrub over her face and her body. Trying to rinse the shampoo out of her hair was a different story, and she wondered if she should have spent the money on a motel room last night—at least then she could have had a hot shower with good water pressure. But she knew the renovations on the house would be costly, and what was left in her bank account after medical expenses and the down payment wasn't exactly extravagant.

She banished the negative thoughts. Although the real

estate agent had warned her that the house needed a lot
of work, Zoe wasn't afraid of rolling up her sleeves and
getting her hands dirty. In fact, she looked forward to it
and even believed the work might be therapeutic for her.
What worried her was the work she couldn't do herself—
the cost of hiring electricians and plumbers and whatever
other tradespeople she might require. Hopefully,
Jessica's husband would be able to tell her exactly what
she needed and maybe make some recommendations.

Another quick glance at her watch warned that she
had less than ten minutes before he was expected to
arrive. She felt the twist of anxiety in her belly as she
pulled on a pair of jeans and a plain white T-shirt. She
didn't know what to expect, what the architect would
suggest, what the cost would be.

She glanced around with a more critical eye. Was it
a pipe dream to believe she could turn this run-down old
home into the proud beauty she knew it had once been?

Well, pipe dream or not, it was hers now—and she
was determined to give it her best shot.

The phone was ringing when Mason walked through
the front door with Rosie. The dog ran across the room
to his water dish and began slurping noisily; Mason
picked up the receiver. "Sullivan."

"You're there. Good." Nick Armstrong sounded
frazzled, which wasn't at all like the man Mason had
known since college and worked with for almost
fifteen years.

"What's up?" he asked.

"I need you to cover an appointment for me this

morning." Then his voice dropped a little as he said, "Hang in, honey. We're almost there."

After a brief moment of confusion, Mason realized the second part of his friend's comment wasn't directed at him. He also noticed that despite the soothing words, there was a note of panic in Nick's tone.

"What's wrong with Jess?" he asked, immediately concerned.

"Her water broke. Only about half an hour ago, but her contractions are already coming hard and strong and way too close together."

Now Mason understood the panic.

Nick and Jess had both waited a long time for the baby they were finally having, and the thought that anything might go wrong at this stage was too horrific to even contemplate.

"Breathe, honey," Nick murmured to his wife.

Mason heard Jess's response—sharp and succinct and completely unlike the cool, poised woman she usually was. That's what having a baby did to normally calm and rational people, he guessed, and was grateful that parenthood wasn't looming anywhere in his future.

Marriage and babies? He shuddered at the thought. Hell, just the suggestion of commitment was enough to make him break out in hives. He'd learned a long time ago how completely love could tear apart a person's life, and he wanted no part of any of it.

His best friend had chosen a different path, however, and Mason was willing to help in any way he could. "Concentrate on your wife," he said. "I'll take care of the business."

"Thanks, Mason."

"Don't worry about it." He winced in automatic sympathy as he heard Jess swear again in the background. "Tell Jess I'll bring her a pint of strawberry ice cream from Walton's later."

"She'll love that," his friend said. "I gotta go now— we're pulling up at the hospital."

"Wait!" Mason said before his friend could disconnect.

"What?"

"When and where is this appointment?"

He took the information from his friend and smiled as he hung up the phone.

This day, he thought, just keeps getting better and better.

Chapter Two

Zoe recognized Mason as soon as she responded to his knock at her front door.

He'd shaved and changed into khaki pants with a shirt and tie rather than the jeans and T-shirt he'd had on earlier, and he didn't have the mammoth beast with him, but the deep blue eyes and sexy smile left her in no doubt that it was her neighbor.

"What are you doing here?" she asked.

"We have an appointment," Mason said, unfazed by the lack of welcome in her question.

"You're Jessica's husband?"

"No." His quick response was confirmed by an emphatic shake of his head. "I'm his business partner. Nick sent me along with his apologies for not being able to meet with you personally. He was on his way to the hospital—it looks like Jessica is going to have the baby today."

It had been apparent to Zoe when she'd been introduced to Jessica Armstrong that the other woman was nearing the end of a pregnancy, but she hadn't realized she was quite that far along.

"I know you were expecting Nick," Mason continued. "But I'm sure you understand that he needed to be with his wife right now."

"Of course," she agreed immediately. But she couldn't help remembering when she'd been in the hospital, without her husband by her side. It hadn't been a happy occasion but the beginning of the end of their marriage.

"Zoe?"

Her attention snapped back to the present.

"Sorry," she apologized automatically. "My thoughts were just wandering."

"Would you rather reschedule when Nick is available?"

"No," she said. "I don't want to reschedule. I just want to know what has to be done to fix this house."

"How much time do you have?"

She narrowed her eyes. "What's that supposed to mean?"

"I'm just suggesting you take a good, hard look around you," Mason said.

She did, and she saw the beauty that had been neglected. The gleam of the hardwood under the layers of dust, the sparkle of the leaded-glass windows beneath the grime, the intricate details of the trims and moldings behind the spider webs. She saw history that needed to be preserved and promise waiting to be fulfilled. But she wasn't comfortable telling him any of those things, so all she said was, "The real estate agent assured me that the building is structurally sound."

"The foundation looks solid," he admitted. "But the roof needs to be replaced, the chimneys need to be re-constructed and the porch rebuilt. And that's just what I could see from the outside. If you really want a home here, it would probably be easier and cheaper to tear this building down and start over again."

It might be easier and cheaper, but it wasn't what she wanted to do. She needed to fix the house—to prove it was valuable and worthwhile despite the damaged parts.

"I'm not interested in easy, and I don't have any il-lusions that it will be cheap, but I want to restore this house," she told him.

He shrugged. "I just wanted to make sure you con-sidered all of the options."

She nodded stiffly, although in her heart she knew she couldn't consider demolition as one of the options. Destroying what was left of this fabulous old building would break her heart all over again.

As they moved through the house, Mason took mea-surements and made notes with brisk efficiency, but he never failed to point out various flaws and defects as they moved from one room to the next through the house. She was frustrated by his incessant negativity and on the verge of telling him she would find another architect when she noticed the inherent contradiction between his actions and his words.

He warned her that the ceiling had sustained some obvious water damage, but his gaze lingered on the pressed tin squares. He claimed that all of the plumbing was horribly outdated, but she'd seen his eyes light up when he'd spotted the old clawfoot tub. And while he was complaining that someone had painted over the mantle of the fireplace, his fingers caressed the hand-carved wood.

"The frames on all of these windows are starting to rot," he said. "They'll have to be replaced."

She sighed, and when she spoke, her words were infused with reluctant resignation. "Maybe you're right. Maybe I should just tear this place down."

His head swiveled toward her, as she'd known it would. His eyes narrowed suspiciously. "Is that what you want to do?"

"I'm starting to believe it's the most logical course of action."

"It is," he said again, after a brief hesitation.

She smiled. "I hope you're a better architect than you are an actor."

"What are you talking about?"

"You can't stand the thought of this beautiful building being destroyed."

"This building is a far cry from beautiful," he told her dryly.

"But it was once, and it can be again, can't it?"

He was silent for a moment before finally conceding, "Maybe."

After so much verbal disparagement, Zoe wasn't willing to let it go at that. "You can see it, can't you?"

she pressed. "You can picture in your mind the way it used to be—the way it should be again?"

"Maybe," he said again. "I've always thought it was a shame that someone didn't step in and do something to save this house before it completely fell apart."

"Why didn't *you*?"

He gave her one of those wry half smiles. "Because as much as I can admire the graceful lines and detailed workmanship, I'm also aware of the time and money needed to fix this place."

"I would think a successful architect would have the necessary resources for the job."

"What I don't have," he warned her, "and anyone in town will tell you the same thing—is the ability to commit to any kind of long-term project."

"Is that why you were baiting me—to determine if I was committed?"

"You had to have dropped a bundle of money already to buy this place," he said. "I'm guessing that's proof of your commitment. I only hope you have a bundle more, because you're going to need it to restore this house properly."

Anxiety twisted knots in her belly. "I'm hoping to do some of the simpler jobs myself. Patching, sanding, painting."

"This house needs a lot more than patching, sanding and painting," he warned.

"I know." And she'd budgeted—hopefully enough— for the other work she knew would be required. "But I want to be involved with the project, not just writing the checks."

His gaze skimmed over her, assessing. "You said you worked at *Images* magazine?"

She nodded. "As a photographer."

"Have you ever done any home renovating before?"

"No," she admitted reluctantly.

"Why did you leave that job to come here?"

"I don't think that's relevant."

"Of course it is," he disagreed.

"I'm committed to this restoration," she said. "That's all that matters."

He studied her for another few seconds before saying, "There are a couple of good general contractors I can recommend. They're local and fair."

She opened her mouth to protest, then decided it wasn't worth arguing with him—she'd rather save her energy for the work that needed to be done. "You can give me their names and numbers after we take a look at the attic."

Mason followed Zoe up the narrow and steep flight of steps that led to the attic. He tried to keep his focus on the job, but he couldn't tear his gaze from the shapely denim-clad butt in front of him. He'd been right about one thing—Zoe Kozlowski cleaned up good.

The blond hair that had been tangled around her face this morning was now tamed into a ponytail, with just the tiniest wisps escaping to frame her oval face. She'd put on a hint of makeup, mascara to darken her lashes, something that added shine to her soft, full lips. Not enough to look done up, but enough to highlight her features.

She was an attractive woman. A lot more attractive than he'd originally thought. Still not his usual type, although he enjoyed women too much to be picky about specifics. And though he enjoyed a lot of women, he never got too close to any one of them except in a strictly physical and always temporary sense.

She turned at the top of the stairs and stepped through an arched doorway and into darkness. He heard the click of a light being switched on, illuminating her slender figure standing in the middle of the attic. He felt the familiar tug of desire any unattached man would feel in the company of a pretty young woman. Emphasis on young, he thought, guessing her age to be somewhere between early- to mid-twenties. Which meant she was too many years younger than he to consider acting on the attraction he felt.

And yet there were shadows in her eyes that hinted she had experienced things beyond her years, a stubborn tilt to her chin that suggested she'd faced some tough challenges—and won. He figured she was a woman with a lot more baggage than the suitcase he'd seen tucked beside the antique couch in the living room, and that was just one more reason not to get involved. While he could respect her strength and determination, Mason didn't do long-term, and he definitely didn't do issues.

He liked women who laughed frequently and easily, women who wanted a good time with no expectations of anything more. He'd thought Erica was such a woman. Until, after less than three months of on-and-off dating that was more "off" than "on," she'd told him it was time he stopped playing around and made a commitment. The night she'd said that was the last time he'd seen her.

He didn't regret ending things with Erica. He couldn't imagine himself in a committed relationship with any woman, and he had no intention of ever falling in love.

But he couldn't deny there were times—times when he was with Nick and Jessica—that he wondered what it would be like to love and be loved so completely. Usually the longing only lasted a moment or two, then he'd remember his father and how losing the woman he loved had started a slow but steady downward spiral that had eventually destroyed him. No, Mason didn't ever want to love like that.

"What do you think?" Zoe asked.

Her question jolted him out of his reverie. He glanced around the enormous room illuminated by a couple of bare bulbs hanging from the steeply sloped ceiling. There were old trunks covered in dust and cobwebs hanging from the rafters. "I think it's dark and dreary."

Some of the light in her eyes faded, making the small space seem darker and drearier still.

"It is now. But if there was a window put in there—" she gestured to the far end "—the room would fill with morning sunlight. It would be perfect for a bedroom and office combined. And there's a bathroom immediately below, so it would be easy enough to bring up the plumbing for an ensuite." She gazed at him hopefully. "Wouldn't it?"

"I'm not sure it would be easy," he warned her. "But, yes, it could be done."

She smiled at him, and he felt as if his breath had backed up in his lungs. He hadn't seen her smile like that before, was unprepared for how positively beautiful she was when her eyes shone, her cheeks glowed. And her mouth—his gaze lingered there, tempted by the sexy curve of those full lips.

He stuffed his hands in his pockets to resist the sudden urge to reach for her, to taste those lips, to test her response. He wondered how it would feel to have a woman look at him like that, to know her smile was intended only for him, the sparkle in her eyes because she was thinking about him.

He gave himself a mental shake, forced himself to focus on what she was saying rather than his imaginative fantasies.

"This will be my space," she decided. "With gleaming hardwood floors, walls painted a cheery yellow, a four-poster bed and—"

Not wanting to think about Zoe tucked away in her bed, he interrupted quickly, "You'll never get a four-poster bed up here. Not the way those stairs curve."

She considered, then sighed. "You're right. Well, the furniture is only details."

"If you're going to tuck yourself away up here, what do you plan to do with the rest of the house?"

"I'm going to open a bed-and-breakfast." She smiled again, her eyes lit up with hope for her grandiose plan.

He hated to dim the sparkle in her eyes again, but someone needed to ground this woman in reality. "There are already a half-dozen bed-and-breakfasts in town," he pointed out. "And even in the height of summer, they're never booked to capacity."

"I'm not looking for busloads of tourists," she said. "But creative marketing and effective advertising will bring enough people here to make the business succeed."

"You never did tell me what brought you here from the big city," he said.

"Obviously I was looking to make some changes in my life."

"Why?"

She narrowed her gaze on him. "Are you this nosy with all of your clients?"

"You're not just a client, you're also my neighbor," he reminded her.

"That's just geography."

"Okay—we'll hold off on the personal revelations until you consider me a friend."

"Friend?" she said, with obvious skepticism.

"Does that seem so impossible to you?"

"Not impossible," she said. "Just surprising."

"Because most men want to skip that part and head straight to the bedroom?"

"Maybe," she admitted hesitantly.

He grinned. "But I'm already in your bedroom."

"So you are." Now she smiled, and again he felt the punch of attraction low in his gut. "But only because you have a really impressive…tape measure."

Zoe left Mason to take his measurements of the attic, heading downstairs on the pretext of needing to dust off the dining room table and a couple of chairs so they could talk about her ideas for the renovations when he was finished. The reality was that she needed some space. The oversized attic that she envisioned as her living quarters seemed far too small when he stood so close to her.

If her purchase of this house had been irrational, her attraction to Mason Sullivan was even more so. He was obviously educated and intelligent, and he was undeniably handsome, but he was also heartache waiting to happen. He was the type of man to whom flirting came as naturally as breathing.

Yeah, she knew the type. And while she couldn't deny she was attracted, she could—and would—refuse to let it lead to anything more. She'd lost too much in the past year-and-a-half, taken too many emotional hits to risk another. And yet, there was something in the way he looked at her that made her feel young and carefree again, that made her want to be the woman she used to be—if only for a little while.

A fantasy, she knew, and a foolish one at that. And when she heard the sound of footsteps at the top of the stairs, she pushed it out of her mind and hastily finished wiping the table.

"I can't even offer you a cup of coffee because I haven't had a chance to get out for groceries yet," she said apologetically.

"That's okay," he said, taking the seat across from her.

She linked her fingers together on top of the table, tried not to let her nervousness show. This was the moment of truth—the moment when she found out if her dreams for this house could be realized or if she'd made a colossal mistake in clearing out most of her savings for the down payment.

He opened his notebook, turned the pages until he found a blank one. His hands were wide, his fingers long, the nails neatly cut. They were strong hands, she imagined, and capable. Hands that would handle any task competently and efficiently, whether sketching a house plan or stroking over a woman's body—

Zoe felt heat infuse her cheeks even as she chastised herself for that incongruous thought.

"You want the attic divided into three separate rooms—a bedroom, bathroom and office," he said, reviewing the instructions she'd given him. "Four bedrooms and two bathrooms on the second level, with each bedroom having access to one of the bathrooms."

She nodded.

"What about this floor?"

"I'm not sure," she admitted. "I don't know that it needs any major changes, but the layout doesn't feel right."

"Because it's been renovated and modernized," he told her. "The space is too open."

"What do you mean?"

"This room—" he gestured to the open flow between the dining and living areas "—is too contemporary for this style of house. You need to break it into individual rooms more appropriate to the era."

As soon as he explained what he meant, she realized he was right. "What do you suggest?"

"A traditional center hall plan with a large foyer as

you come through the front door. With this whole side as the dining area so that you can set up several smaller tables for your guests, connecting doors to the kitchen, and, on the other side, a parlor in the front, maybe a library behind it."

The possibility hadn't occurred to her, but now that he'd mentioned it, she was intrigued by the idea.

"You could build bookcases into the walls on either side of the fireplace, add a few comfortable chairs for guests to relax and read."

She could picture it exactly as he described and smiled at the cozy image that formed in her mind. "You're really good at this."

"It's my job."

She shook her head. "I'd say it's a passion."

He glanced away, as if her insight made him uncomfortable, and shrugged. "I've always loved old houses."

"Why?" she asked, genuinely curious.

"Because of the history and uniqueness of each structure. Don't tell Nick, or he might start looking for a new partner, but I actually enjoy renovating old buildings more than designing new ones. It's an incredible experience—revealing what has been hidden, uncovering the beauty so often unseen."

She didn't want to like him. It was awkward enough that she was attracted to him, even though she was determined to ignore the attraction. But listening to him talk, knowing he felt the same way she did about this old house, she felt herself softening toward him. "It must be enormously satisfying to love what you do."

"The key is to do what you love," he told her.

She nodded, understanding, because there had been a time not so very long ago that she'd done just that. But somewhere along the road that love had faded, too.

"Isn't there anything you're passionate about?" he asked.

She expected the question to be accompanied by a flirtatious wink or suggestive grin, but his expression was serious, almost intense. As if he really wanted to know, as if he was interested in what mattered to her.

"This house," she answered automatically.

"That's obvious," he said. "But what fired your passion before you came to Pinehurst?"

She shook her head, refusing to look back, to think about everything she'd left behind. "Can we focus on the house right now?"

"Okay."

But the depth of his scrutiny belied his easy response, and she didn't relax until he'd turned his attention back to his notebook.

"Where did you want to put your darkroom?" he asked.

The question made her realize she'd relaxed too soon.

"I don't need a darkroom," she said.

"There's plenty of room in the basement," he continued as if she hadn't spoken. "And it's certainly dark down there. Or you could convert the laundry room.

"I designed a home for Warren Crenshaw and his wife, Nancy. They're both nature photographers—not professionally, but it's a hobby they share. We put a darkroom right off their bedroom."

"I don't need a darkroom," she repeated tightly. "I'm not a photographer anymore."

"Whether or not you have a camera in your hand, you're still a photographer. It's the kind of thing that's in your blood—like designing houses is in mine."

She shook her head, swallowed around the lump in her throat. "I left that part of my life in Manhattan."

He hesitated, as if there was something more he wanted to say, but then her cell phone rang.

"Excuse me," she said, pushing her chair away from the table.

She dug the phone out of her purse, connecting the call before it patched through to her voice mail. "Hello."

"Where are you?" Scott asked without preamble.

The unexpected sound of his voice gave her a jolt, and made her heart ache just a little. The question, on the other hand, and the tone, annoyed her. "Why are you calling?"

"I just wanted to check in, see how you were doing."

She walked toward the window, away from where Mason was still seated at the table. "I'm fine."

"I'd be more likely to believe that if you were where you said you'd be."

"I *am* in Pinehurst," she told him.

"You said you'd be staying with Claire."

"Not forever."

He sighed. "She told me you were thinking about buying a house."

She frowned at that, wondering why her friend would have told Scott anything. But she couldn't blame Claire because she knew, better than anyone, how charming and persuasive he could be. "And?"

"Buying a house is a major decision," he said gently. "And you've had a tough year."

"Too late."

She heard his groan, fought back a smile.

"It was completely irrational and impulsive," she admitted. "I saw the sign on the lawn, contacted the agent and made an offer."

"Please tell me you at least had a home inspection done."

Now she did smile. Reasonable, practical Scott Cowan would never understand the need deep within her heart that had compelled her to buy this house. "A home inspector would have told me it needed a lot of work," she said, not admitting that she'd been given a copy of the report from an inspection done on the property just a few months earlier. "I already know that."

"Christ, Zoe. Have you gone completely off the deep end?"

"That seems to be the general consensus," she agreed.

"Let me contact my lawyers," he said. "Maybe there's a way to undo the transaction."

"No," she said quickly.

"What do you mean 'no'?"

She sighed. "I mean, I don't want it undone. I want this house."

"You could be making a very big mistake," he warned.

She knew he was right. But she'd spent the better part of her twenty-nine years doing the smart thing, the safe thing—and she'd still been unprepared for the curves that life had thrown her way. Even if buying this house turned out to be a mistake, it would be *her* mistake.

"Why should you care?" she challenged. "You walked out on me, remember?"

"You kicked me out."

He was right, she had to admit. But only because she couldn't continue to live with him the way things had been.

"Does it matter?" she asked wearily. "The end result is the same."

"I'll always care about you, Zoe."

And that might have been enough to hold them together if other obstacles hadn't got in the way. She rubbed her hand over her chest, trying to assuage an ache she wasn't sure would ever go away. "Was that the only reason you called?"

"When's your next appointment with Dr. Allison?"

She felt the sting of tears. If he'd been half as concerned about her twelve or even six months ago, what had been left of their relationship might not have fallen apart.

"I have to go, Scott."

Before he could say anything else, she disconnected the call. She heard the telltale scrape of chair legs against the hardwood floor and blinked the moisture from her eyes.

She felt Mason's hand on her shoulder, gently but firmly turning her to face him. "Zoe?"

She didn't—couldn't—look at him. She just needed half a minute to pull herself together, to find the cloak of feigned confidence and false courage that she'd learned to wrap around herself so no one would see how shaky and scared she was feeling inside.

"Who was that on the phone?" he asked.

She took a deep, steadying breath and prepared to dodge the question. After all, it was none of his business. She hardly knew this man; she certainly didn't owe him any explanations.

But when she looked up at him, she realized he wasn't trying to pry or interfere. He'd asked the question because he knew she was upset, and he was concerned. In the past eighteen months, she'd withdrawn into herself. She'd been let down by people she'd counted on, disappointed by friends who hadn't been there for her. Except for her almost daily phone calls to Claire, she'd been on her own. She'd learned to rely on herself, to need no one else.

After only a few days in this small town, she knew that was one of the reasons she'd come here—because she didn't want to live the rest of her life alone. She wanted—needed—friends to care about and who would care about her.

So she took what she hoped was the first step in that direction and answered his question honestly.

"That was my husband."

Chapter Three

*H*usband?

Mason's head reeled. Zoe's announcement had caught him completely unaware. And delivered as it was, in that soft, sexy voice, the punch was even more unexpected.

It took a minute for his brain to absorb this startling bit of information that—at least for him—changed the whole equation.

Zoe was married.

He couldn't have said why her revelation surprised him so much, or why it left him feeling oddly disappointed. He only knew that he needed to stop thinking of this woman as his sexy new neighbor and focus on the fact that she was someone's wife.

Damn.

Zoe might not be his usual type, but he found himself drawn to her regardless. There was just something about her that intrigued him—enough so that, in the brief time between their first meeting that morning and his return for their scheduled appointment, he'd found himself looking forward to spending time with her, getting to know her. And maybe, eventually, moving toward a more intimate and personal relationship with her.

Of course, that was all before he'd learned she was married.

It was his own fault for letting his fantasies get ahead of him, and he silently cursed himself for that now. His hand dropped away and he took a step back.

She gazed at him uncertainly as she folded her arms over her chest. Her cell phone was still clutched in her hand—her left hand. He noted that fact along with the absence of any rings on her fingers.

"You don't wear a wedding band," he noted.

Of course he knew that not everyone did. But he sensed that she was the type who would, that if she'd made a commitment to someone, she would display the evidence of that commitment. Then again, he'd been wrong about assuming she was uninvolved, so maybe he was wrong about this, too.

She shook her head and moved back to the dining room, returning to the chair she'd vacated to answer the call. "No, I don't wear a ring. Not anymore. Not since…that is, I'm—I mean we're—getting a divorce."

"Oh," he said, as he absorbed this second unexpected—but more welcome—revelation. And then he felt like a heel, because he was relieved to know that her marriage had fallen apart so that he didn't need to feel guilty for fantasizing about a married woman.

"We're just waiting for the final papers to come through," she admitted.

"I'm sorry," he said lamely.

She shrugged. "It happens."

Yeah, he knew that it did. He also knew that a break-up was never as easy as she implied, even if it was the right choice.

"How long were you married?" he asked.

"Almost nine years."

He stared at the woman who didn't look like she was twenty-five. "Did you get married while you were still in high school?"

She smiled at that. "Fresh out of college."

"How old were you when you went to college?"

"I'm twenty-nine," she told him.

And he was thirty-seven—which meant there weren't as many years between them as he'd originally suspected, but there was still the barrier of her marriage. And even if her divorce papers came through tomorrow, she was obviously still hung up on her husband. Her evident distress over his phone call was proof of that.

"What did your soon-to-be-ex-husband want?" he asked. "Did you take off with his coffeemaker or something like that?"

"No, nothing like that. We actually had a very civilized settlement."

"Then why was he calling you now?"

"He heard from a friend of mine that I bought a house and wanted to tell me he thought it was a mistake."

"Did you tell him it was none of his business?"

"Yes," she said. "But after nine years of marriage— and not just living together, but working together, too— some habits are hard to break."

"Is he a photographer, too?"

"No. He's the senior fashion editor at *Images*."

"Is that why you left Manhattan?"

She shook her head. "It's a big enough city that I could have stayed, found a new apartment, a new job, and probably have never seen him again if I didn't want to. But everything just seemed so inexplicably woven together there. I needed to get away from all of it, to make a fresh start somewhere else."

"Well, you picked a good place for that."

"Speaking from experience?"

His surprise must have shown, because she smiled.

"Maybe I didn't peg you quite as quickly as you did me," she said, "but the more I listen to you talk, the more I hear just the subtlest hint of a drawl."

"You can take a boy out of the south, but you can't take the south out of the boy," he mused.

"How far south?"

"Beaufort, South Carolina."

"What brought you up here?"

"I came north to go to college, met Nick Armstrong there, came to Pinehurst for a visit one summer and decided to stay up here to go into business with him."

"Do you go home very often?"

"This is my home now."

"Don't you have any family left in Beaufort?"

He shook his head again. "There's just me and my brother, Tyler, and he's living up here now, too."

"No wife or ex-wife?" she wondered.

He shuddered at the thought. "No."

"Well, that was definite enough."

"Not that I'm opposed to the institution of marriage. In fact, I was the best man when Nick got married." He grinned. "Both times."

"He was married to someone before Jessica?"

"To your real estate agent actually."

Now *that* came as a surprise to Zoe.

"I don't know Jessica very well, obviously," she said. "But the way she talked about Nick, I got the impression they'd been together forever."

"They've been in love forever," he agreed. "Had a brief romance when they were younger, then went their separate ways and found each other again only last year."

"Doesn't that seem strange to you?"

"It's a small town," he reminded her. "And Nick's ex was remarried long before Jess ever came back to town."

Zoe thought about the possibility of Scott marrying again, and wondered if she could ever bring herself to be friends with her ex-husband's new wife. Then she decided it was a moot point. He was out of her life; she'd moved away; they'd both moved on.

She felt the familiar ache of loss, but it wasn't as

sharp or as strong as it once had been. She'd finally accepted that he couldn't be what she'd needed him to be any more than she could be what he'd wanted. And while her body would always carry the scars of what had finally broken their marriage, she realized that her heart was finally starting to heal.

Mason didn't know anything about babies, but he couldn't deny that the pink bundle in Jessica's arms was kind of cute. Elizabeth Theresa Armstrong had soft blond fuzz on her head, tiny ears and an even tinier nose. She yawned, revealing toothless gums, then blinked and looked at her mother through the biggest, bluest eyes he'd ever seen.

"She's a beauty, Jess."

The new mother beamed. "She really is, isn't she?"

"Absolutely," he agreed. "Just like her mother."

Jess chuckled. "Actually, she looks exactly like Nick's baby pictures."

"No kidding?" He glanced at the proud father standing by the window. "Let's hope she has better luck as she grows up."

His partner chose to ignore the comment, asking instead, "How was your appointment with Ms. Kozlowski?"

"It was…interesting," he said, unconsciously echoing Zoe's description of their initial meeting. He carried the vase of flowers he'd brought for Jessica over to the windowsill to join the other arrangements that were already there. "The house needs a lot of work."

"What did you think of the owner?" Jess asked.

"I think she needs her head examined," he said. "And so do you, for not trying to talk her out of buying that place."

"No one could have talked her out of it."

Mason had caught only a glimpse of Zoe's steely determination and guessed Jess was probably right.

"You still should have tried," he said, setting the pint of promised ice cream and a plastic spoon on the table beside her bed.

"If she hadn't bought it, we wouldn't have got the referral," Nick pointed out. "And it would've killed you to watch another architect put his hands all over that house."

"So long as you keep your hands on the *house*," Jess said.

Nick lifted an eyebrow in silent question.

Mason shook his head. "She's not my type."

"Is she female?" his friend asked dryly.

"A very attractive female," Jess interjected. "Who's new in town and doesn't need to be hit on by the first guy she meets."

"I was the consummate professional," Mason assured her, and it was true—even if he'd had some very personal and inappropriate thoughts about her.

The baby squirmed, and when Jess started to shift her to the other arm, Nick swooped in and picked her up.

"Do you want to hold her?" he asked his friend.

Mason took an instinctive step in retreat. "No, um, thanks, but, um…"

Jess took advantage of having her hands free to reach for the container of ice cream. As she pried open the lid, she commented, "I've never seen you back away from a woman before, Mason."

"My experience is with babes, not babies." He felt a quick spurt of panic as his friend deposited the infant in his arms and stepped away, leaving the tiny fragile bundle in his awkward grasp. Then he gazed at the angelic face again and his heart simply melted.

He reminded himself that he didn't want what his friends had. Marriage, children, family—they were the kind of ties he didn't dare risk. Yet somehow, these friends had become his extended family.

He'd had a family once, a long time ago. Parents who had loved one another and doted on their two sons. He'd been fourteen years old when his mother got sick; Tyler had been only ten. Elaine Sullivan had valiantly fought the disease for almost two years, but everyone had known it was only a matter of time. The ravages of the illness had been obvious in her sunken cheeks, dull eyes and pasty skin.

Gord Sullivan had fallen apart when he'd realized the woman he loved was dying. Unable to deal with the ravages of her illness, he'd looked for solace in whiskey—and other women. Mason had never figured out if it was denial or some kind of coping mechanism. He only knew that his father's abandonment had hurt his mother more than the disease that had eaten away at her body.

Four years after they'd lowered Elaine's coffin into the ground, her husband was laid to rest beside her. The doctors blamed his death on cirrhosis of the liver. Mason knew his father had really died of a broken heart.

It was a hard but unforgettable lesson, and when

he'd buried his father, Mason had promised himself he wouldn't ever let himself love that deeply or be that vulnerable. He refused to risk that kind of loss again.

And yet, when he looked at Nick and Jess and their new baby, the obvious love they felt for one another evident in every look that passed between them, he found himself wanting to believe that happy endings were possible. He wanted to believe his friends would be luckier than his parents.

One of the drawbacks of buying the house and its contents, Zoe realized, was having to *clean* the house *and* its contents. After Beatrice Hadfield died, her grandson hadn't removed anything from the house, which meant there was a lot of cleaning *up* to do before she could even begin to tackle the dust and cobwebs that had taken up residence in the vacant house over the past couple of years.

She took down all the curtains and stripped the beds, then spent half a day and a couple rolls of quarters at The Laundry Basket in town. She emptied out closets and dressers and shelves and cupboards and packed up dozens of boxes for charity. She sorted through cabinets full of china and stemware, tossing out anything that was cracked or chipped. When she was done, she still had enough pieces left to serve a five-course meal to twenty guests.

It took her three days to get through the rooms on the first two floors, then three more days to sort through everything in the attic. There were trunks of old clothes, shelves of old books and boxes and boxes of papers and photos. She was tempted to just toss everything—it would certainly be the quickest and easiest solution—but her conscience wouldn't let her throw out anything without first knowing what it was.

She found letters and journals and lost a whole day reading through them. She felt guilty when she opened the cover of what she quickly realized was a personal journal of Beatrice Hadfield's from some fifty years back, but the remorse was eclipsed by curiosity as the woman's bold writing style and recitation of details quickly drew Zoe into the world in which she'd lived back then—and the passionate affair the woman had had with a writer who had rented a room in the house for several months one summer. A writer who had gone on to win several awards for plays, more than one of which Zoe had seen on Broadway.

On the morning of the seventh day in her new home, there was still cleaning to be done and she'd run out of supplies. So she grabbed her keys and purse and headed into town for what was intended as a quick stop at Anderson's Hardware. She didn't anticipate that being a newcomer in a town where almost everyone knew everyone else would make her a curiosity.

She'd barely managed to put the first items—a bucket and mop—in her cart when a tall, white-haired man approached.

"I'm Harry Anderson," he said. "You must be the young lady who bought the Hadfield place."

She nodded. "Zoe Kozlowski."

"Welcome to Pinehurst, Zoe." He smiled. "Is there anything I can help you find?"

"I just needed to pick up a few cleaning supplies."

She thought she was capable of browsing and making her own selections, but Harry Anderson clearly had other ideas. Instead of leaving her to her shopping, he guided her around the store, asking questions and making suggestions along the way.

Other customers came and went, each one exchanging greetings with the store owner who, in turn, insisted on introducing her. While he was occupied with Sue Walton—"her family owns the ice-cream parlor down the street"—she steered her cart toward the checkout.

She wasn't sure she had everything she'd need, but she had at least enough to get started and she really wanted to get back home and do just that. She was paying for her purchases when Tina Stilwell, her real estate agent, came into the store.

"I thought that was your car outside," Tina said to Zoe, then she stood on tiptoes to kiss the cheek of the man beside her, "Hello, Uncle Harry."

"Hello, darling."

"Did you forget about our lunch plans?" she asked Zoe.

Zoe glanced at her watch, as surprised to see that it was almost lunchtime as she was by the other woman's reference to plans she knew they'd never made. "I guess I did."

"Well, you girls go on, then," Harry said. "I don't want to keep you any longer."

"Thanks for your help, Mr. Anderson," Zoe said.

The old man smiled at her. "It was real nice meeting you, Zoe. Good luck with that house."

"Thanks," she said.

Then, to Tina, as they walked out of the store, "And thank *you*."

Tina smiled. "My uncle Harry is a darling man with far too much time on his hands."

"I can't believe I was in there an hour," Zoe said. "I've never spent an hour in a hardware store in my entire life."

"You've never lived in Pinehurst before. This town operates on a whole different schedule than the rest of the world."

"I miss Manhattan already," she muttered, unlocking the trunk of her car to deposit her purchases inside.

The other woman chuckled. "What do you miss? The crowds, the noise or the chaos?"

"All of the above." She closed the trunk. "But I think what I miss most is the anonymity."

"I felt the same way when I first moved here from Boston."

Zoe smiled. "Is there anyone living in this town who actually grew up here?"

"Of course," Tina said. "I'll fill you in on all the local characters over lunch."

She glanced at her watch again. "I really have a ton of things to do at the house."

"Have you eaten?"

"No," she admitted, belatedly realizing that she also needed to restock her dwindling food supply.

"Then let's go," Tina said. "Because if we don't show up at Freda's, Uncle Harry will know before the end of the day that I lied to him."

And so she ended up having lunch with Tina at the

popular little café. And she enjoyed it, far more than she expected to. It had been a long time since she'd shared a simple meal and easy conversation with a friend. And though she didn't know Tina very well, she already considered her a friend—one of the first she'd made in Pinehurst.

Then she thought of Mason, and wondered whether he might be another. She'd been thinking about him a lot since their initial meeting a week earlier—probably too much—so she put those thoughts aside and dug into her spinach salad.

When Zoe finally got home after lunch and grocery shopping, she felt as though she'd already put in a full day and hadn't even begun to tackle the dust and dirt. She shoved a bucket under the kitchen tap and turned on the water, thinking that it would have been nice to hire a cleaning service to come in and scrub the place from top to bottom. But that was a luxury she couldn't afford—especially not when she had time on her hands and nothing else to do.

Still, it was almost nine o'clock before she decided to hang up her mop for the night. Although she was physically exhausted, her mind was unsettled, her thoughts preoccupied with everything yet to be done. She decided a nice cup of tea would help her relax and get some sleep.

After the kettle had boiled, she carried her mug out to the porch and settled into an old weathered Adirondack chair. She lifted her feet to prop them on the railing, then dropped them quickly when the wood creaked and swayed. Instead, she folded her legs beneath her on the chair and cradled her mug between her palms.

The darkness of the nights still surprised her, with no streetlights or neon signs to illuminate the blackness of night. There was only the moon, about three-quarters full tonight, and an array of stars unlike anything she'd ever seen. She breathed deeply, filling her lungs with the cool, fresh air, and smiled. It was beautiful, peaceful, and exactly what she needed.

At least until she heard a thump on the porch and registered the bump against her arm half a second before she felt the shock of hot tea spilling down the front of her shirt and a disgustingly familiar wet tongue sweeping across her mouth.

She sputtered and pushed the hairy beast aside.

"Rosie, down."

He sat, panting happily beside her chair.

Zoe resisted the urge to scream, asking instead, in a carefully controlled voice, "Where is your master?"

The beast tilted his head, as if trying to understand the question, but—of course—made no response to it.

"Maybe you're smarter than he is," she said. "Do you understand the word *by-law?*"

The beast merely cocked his head from one side to the next.

"Or *dog pound?*"

He barked, but then he licked her hand, clearly proving his ignorance.

"How about *leash?*" she asked in a deliberately friendly tone.

The beast dropped to his belly on the porch, covered his ears with his paws and whimpered.

Zoe exhaled a frustrated breath and untangled her

legs. She set the now half-empty cup of tea on the arm of the chair and stood up. "Let's go," she said.

Rosie danced in ecstatic circles around her, nearly tripping her on the stairs.

It was the start of the ninth inning in a tie game when Mason heard knocking. He scowled at the door, his eyes still glued to the television. It was early in the season, but his commitment to his Yankees was resolute. Unfortunately, so was the pounding.

He swore under his breath as he pushed himself off the couch. The lead-off batter singled to right field and Mason pulled open the door. The sight of the woman on the other side was so unexpected—and so unexpectedly appealing in a pair of yoga-style pants that sat low on her hips and a skimpy white tank top—he actually forgot about the ballgame playing out on the fifty-two-inch screen behind him.

"This beast is a menace," Zoe said tightly.

He winced and glanced at the animal sitting obediently at her side. "What did he do now?"

"What did he do?" she echoed indignantly. "Look at me."

He took her words as an invitation, allowing his eyes to move over her—from the slightly lopsided ponytail on top of her head to the pink-painted toenails on her feet—lingering momentarily at some of the more interesting places in between.

"This—" she gestured to the stain on the front of her shirt that he'd thought was a flower "—was a cup of very hot tea."

"It's...pink."

Her cheeks seemed to take on the same color.

"It's herbal tea," she said. "Raspberry. But that's not the point."

"Of course not," he agreed solemnly.

Her eyes narrowed. "The point is that you were going to keep him on a leash."

Rosie tucked her paws over her ears and whimpered.

Zoe rolled her eyes in disbelief. "You've obviously taught him to react whenever he hears that word. Why can't you teach him to stay off my property?"

"I think he has a crush on you."

She sent him a look of patent disbelief.

"I'm not kidding," he told her. "He's never wandered away from the backyard without me before."

"I find that hard to believe."

"It's true. And I really am sorry about—" his gaze fell to the pink stain on the front of her shirt and the tempting feminine curves beneath it "—your tea."

She crossed her arms over her chest. "I'm hopeful it will wash out."

"Then will we be forgiven?"

"Maybe the dog," she said. "Not you. You should know better than to let him roam free."

He scratched the top of Rosie's head. "He's just very affectionate."

"His affection is wreaking havoc on my wardrobe."

"You're welcome to come over anytime to use my washer and dryer, if you want."

"Thanks," she said. "But I'll stick with The Laundry Basket."

"That's right," he said. "You don't like to be on top of your neighbors."

Her eyes narrowed on him.

He grinned. "Or was it that you didn't like your neighbors on top?"

"Maybe it's just some neighbors in particular that I have a problem with."

"You'll get over it," he said confidently. "Pinehurst is too small a town to hold a grudge against anyone for long."

"I'll give it my best shot," she told him.

He couldn't help but chuckle. "I think I'm going to enjoy getting to know you, Zoe Kozlowski."

"Maybe another time," she said. "Right now, I want to get home. I have a ton of things to do in the morning."

"Wait," he said, as she turned away.

She hesitated with obvious reluctance.

"Let me walk you back."

"I don't need an escort."

"I know you don't," he agreed, sliding his feet into his shoes. "But it's a nice night for a walk and I don't want you going home mad."

"I wouldn't count on your company changing my disposition," she warned him.

He grinned. "I'll chance it."

"What about the beast?"

He glanced regretfully at the animal by his feet. Rosie was looking up at him and thumping his tail in eager anticipation. As much as Mason regretted having to punish him, the dog had to learn that there were consequences to his actions. "Stay."

The bundle of fur immediately sprawled on the floor,

settling his chin on his front paws and looking up at his master with sorrow-filled eyes.

Mason ignored the guilt that tugged at him as he closed the door.

"Why do you call him that?" he asked.

"What?"

"The beast."

"Because he is one."

"You're going to hurt his feelings," he warned.

She turned, a reluctant smile tugging at the corners of her mouth. "His or yours?"

"You have a beautiful smile, Zoe."

He was disappointed, although not surprised, that his comment succeeded in erasing any trace of it.

"Flattery is not going to get you or your dog off the hook."

"Why are you assuming that I have an ulterior motive?"

"Because everyone does."

He took her hand, rubbed his thumb over the back of her knuckles. She didn't tug away, but he could tell by the wariness in her eyes that she wanted to.

"Have dinner with me," he said impulsively.

"I already ate."

"I didn't mean tonight."

She hesitated. "I'm going to be busy with the house for quite a while."

"You still have to eat," he pointed out.

"I know but—"

"Tomorrow night," he interrupted what he was sure would be a refusal. "We'll barbecue some steaks, open a bottle of wine—"

"I really don't—"

"—and talk about the plans for your house," he continued.

The rest of her protest died on her lips. "My house?"

He couldn't help but smile. Every woman had a weakness—he'd just never before met one whose soft spot was a pile of crumbling bricks.

"I had some concerns about the kitchen renovation I thought we should discuss before I draw up the plans."

"So this would be a…business meeting?"

"We can call it whatever you want."

She frowned at that. "I'm not ready to start dating again."

"And I don't date married women," he told her.

"Okay." She smiled now, clearly relieved. "In that case, yes—I'd like to have dinner with you tomorrow night."

"Good." He released her hand when they reached her back porch. "Seven o'clock?"

She nodded. "Sounds good."

He watched her walk up the steps, appreciating the toned length of her legs, the round curve of her butt, the gentle sway of her hips. Yeah, she had some nice moves and an appealing look, and it occurred to him that though he was sorry she was going through a divorce, he was glad she wouldn't be married for very much longer.

Chapter Four

There were times that Zoe really missed her morning cup of coffee. Saturday morning was one of those times.

After her evening visit from Rosie and her confrontation with Mason, she'd had a lot on her mind and found sleep eluded her for most of the night. Some of her preoccupation was caused by worries about the house, about the concerns stirred up by her recent conversation with her ex-husband. She hadn't expected that he would accept her plans or understand her choices. Somewhere along the line, their lives had started to take different paths, until—at the end—she'd wondered how they'd ever believed they would be together forever.

Still, his doubts nagged at her, his implication that

she was in over her head worried her. There had been a time when she would have laughed at such naysayers, because she was strong and determined and invincible. Now she knew differently.

But she'd managed to put those concerns aside fairly easily. A lot more easily than her thoughts about Mason Sullivan.

He was, she knew, the real reason she'd been awake through so much of the night. Because she'd been thinking about him, and worrying about the long-dormant feelings he stirred inside her.

She was attracted to him—there was no denying that. There was something about those blue eyes and the easy smile that warmed her blood in a way that made her realize she'd been cold for too long. If the sudden attraction she felt surprised her, it worried her even more. She hadn't anticipated experiencing those kind of feelings again, and she didn't know what to do about them.

But she did know that daydreaming about Mason wasn't going to get her work done. In fact, fantasizing about the sexy architect could only complicate her life at a time when she was trying to keep things simple— at least on a personal level. And so she resolved to put everyone and everything out of her mind, crank up the radio and get the house cleaned.

She'd just plugged in her boom box when the doorbell rang. She wasn't expecting any company, but her heart skipped a beat at the thought that it might be her closest neighbor stopping by. She was surprised—but not dis-appointed—to find her best friend on the porch.

She threw open the door to give Claire a hug before asking, "What are you doing here?"

"What kind of a greeting is that?" her friend chided.

"The greeting of someone who thought you would be on your way to Pennsylvania this weekend for your son's baseball tournament."

"That's what I thought, too," Claire admitted. "But the Hawks lost two of their first three games so they didn't advance to the finals. Instead of Laurel and I heading to Scranton today, Rob and Jason came home last night."

"He must be so disappointed."

"Who?" Her friend's lips curved. "Jason or Rob?"

Zoe smiled back. "I meant Jason, although I imagine it was a blow to the coach, too."

"It was," Claire agreed. "But considering that they went undefeated all the way to the playoffs last year, they were overdue to lose a game—or two."

"Well, I'm sorry for Jason—and Rob—but I'm happy for me," Zoe said. "I've been so anxious for you to see inside this place."

"I'm sorry I couldn't get over last week when you got the keys, but things have been crazy at school and Laurel's had extra music lessons to prep for her upcoming recital and—"

"You don't have to apologize for having a life," Zoe said.

"You mean for having children who have lives," her friend corrected. "I'm just the cook and chauffeur."

She smiled again. "I'm just glad you're here now and with—" she eyed the take-out tray in Claire's hand "—dare I hope that's coffee?"

"It is. I know you mostly gave up caffeine—"

"*Mostly* being the key word. And I was sorely regretting not having any on hand this morning."

"Then you can take this," Claire said, passing her the tray, "while I go get the rest of the stuff from the car."

"The rest of the stuff" turned out to be two armloads of housewarming gifts. There was a ficus plant in a brass pot with a big red bow around it, a bottle of Zoe's favorite chardonnay, a handful of glossy magazines featuring Victorian home designs and renovations and a Tupperware container filled with homemade chocolate chip cookies.

"Oh—and one more thing," Claire said, pulling a camera and several canisters of film out of her purse. "Rob finally bought a digital, so this one was just sitting around. It's one of those point-and-shoot models designed for amateurs like me, but I thought it would serve the purpose."

"What purpose might that be?" Zoe asked in a deliberately casual tone.

"Before and after pictures," her friend said, sliding the camera across the countertop toward her. "So that you can show people what it used to look like after the renovations are complete."

"That's a good idea," she acknowledged, but reached for one of the paper cups instead of the Canon.

Claire took the other cup, indicating a willingness to let the subject drop—at least for now.

"Let's go into the dining room," Zoe suggested, leading the way. "You can tell me if the table and chairs are real antiques."

"You got the furniture with the house?"

"I got *everything* with the house, and I've spent the past week trying to figure out what to do with it all. But I'm glad for the furniture because without it, we'd be sitting on the floor."

"Well, knowing how old Beatrice Hadfield was when she passed away, I'd bet you did get honest-to-goodness antiques," Claire said.

"You knew Mrs. Hadfield?"

"She was my math teacher in high school. And my mother's math teacher when she was in high school." Claire frowned. "Maybe my grandmother's, too."

Zoe laughed. "She wasn't *that* old."

"Close enough." Her friend smiled. "It's so good to hear you laugh, Zoe. And to see you looking so happy."

"I'm feeling pretty happy. And a little overwhelmed when I let myself think too hard about everything that needs to be done around here," she admitted. "But mostly happy."

"I'm happy that you've decided to stay in Pinehurst."

"But?" Zoe prompted.

"But I'm worried that you've rushed into this. That six months from now, you'll regret walking away—not just from the magazine, but from your whole life in New York City."

She shook her head. "I don't have a life in New York City anymore."

Claire hesitated a moment before asking, "Have you talked to Scott since you've been here?"

"He called last week."

"I thought he might." Claire winced. "I didn't realize

you hadn't told him about the house, and when I mentioned it, he seemed a little, uh, concerned."

Zoe smiled. "You mean he went ballistic?"

"Something like that."

"Funny how much he cares so much about what I'm doing now that we're almost divorced."

"Are you doing okay with that?" Claire asked gently.

"I am," she assured her friend. "I'm sad, of course, that our marriage ended the way it did, but I have no doubts that it was over. And, for the first time in a long time, I'm looking forward to the future. I'm excited about this project, thrilled to finally have a sense of direction and a purpose."

"And your purpose now is to operate a bed-and-breakfast?"

She nodded. "Are you going to try to talk me out of this—tell me I'm crazy to even consider it?"

"Nope. Because you're one of the smartest, strongest, gutsiest women I know, and I don't believe there's anything you can't do."

Her friend spoke so sincerely that the words brought tears to Zoe's eyes.

Then Claire, understanding that something needed to be done to lighten the mood before they both ending up bawling, added, "Although I'd suggest you at least run a dusting cloth and vacuum around here before you open the door to guests."

Zoe managed to smile at that. "I think it will be a while before I open the door to anyone but my closest friends."

"That's what I figured—and the reason I'm dressed like this." She indicated her T-shirt and leggings.

"You brought me coffee and you came to help me clean? You really are a true friend."

"My motives aren't completely altruistic," Claire admitted. "I was in desperate need of an excuse to get out of the house after Rob's mother showed up this morning for an unexpected visit."

"Then I'll have to thank Rob's mother if I ever meet her, because I'm really glad you're here."

"Me, too." Claire finished off her coffee, set her empty cup aside and stood up. "Now let's tackle some dirt."

"I can't believe how horribly neglected this place was," Zoe said when they finally decided to take a break for lunch.

"It's been vacant for almost two years," Claire reminded her. "And Mrs. Hadfield probably hadn't managed to do a thorough cleaning for several years prior to that."

Zoe spread butter on bread for sandwiches. "It's sad to think that she lived in this big old house all by herself for so long. And died alone."

"Her grandson tried to get her to move out to California," Claire told her. "But she refused to move away from the only home she'd ever known, especially to some godforsaken place so overrun with hippies and movie stars it would only be fitting for it to fall into the ocean."

Zoe chuckled at that as she layered slices of turkey and Havarti. "Sounds like she was quite a character."

"That she was. And always sticking her nose into all her neighbors' business." She smiled her thanks as she took the plate and bottle of water that Zoe passed to her.

"Speaking of neighbors," she continued on her way into the dining room. "Have you met Mason Sullivan yet?"

Zoe put down the sandwich she'd just picked up and stared across the table in disbelief. "You know him?"

Her friend smiled. "Honey, I'd bet there isn't a single woman in this town who doesn't know Mason Sullivan."

"You're not single."

Claire's smile widened. "I used to be."

Zoe decided she wasn't going to ask—she really didn't want to know. Instead, she said, "Yes, I've met Mason. He's going to draft some renovation plans for me."

"Hmm." Claire chewed on her sandwich. "Has he hit on you yet?"

"Well, he seemed extremely interested in my plumbing and wiring."

Her friend laughed. "And did you check out his…structure?"

She couldn't lie. Nor could she prevent the smile that curved her lips. "I can confidently state that there were no obvious flaws."

Claire studied her across the table for a long moment, smiling smugly until Zoe couldn't stand it anymore.

"What?" she finally demanded.

"I was just noticing the intriguing color in your cheeks. In fact, if I didn't know better, I might almost suspect that you were blushing," her friend teased.

Zoe scowled. "I'm too old and jaded for that."

"You're not even thirty yet."

"Getting close," she said, remembering a time when

she'd dreaded the milestone, hated the thought of growing older. Now she looked forward to it and intended to cherish every day on the journey.

"Which means you should be old enough and wise enough to appreciate that you've been given a second chance—not just at life, but for love."

"Right now, I'm just taking things one step at a time," Zoe said lightly.

"Buying this house was a good first step. Getting to know your neighbor a little better could be the second."

"One step at a time," she said again.

"Okay," Claire relented. "If you don't want to talk about Mason, let's talk about dinner."

"We've just finished lunch."

"I know, but Rob said he would throw together a broccoli and chicken casserole tonight and asked if you wanted to join us."

She was touched by the offer, pleased that her friend's husband would think to include her in their family plans and apprehensive about declining the invitation.

"Thanks," she said, picking up her plate and empty bottle to take them back into the kitchen. "But, um, actually, I have other plans."

She heard the scrape of chair legs on the floor as Claire followed her. "You moved into town just over a week ago and you already have plans with someone other than me?"

"I thought you were going to be away all weekend," Zoe reminded her. "But I can cancel and—"

"You absolutely will *not* cancel," Claire said firmly. "But you will tell me what your plans are."

"I'm having dinner with Mason," she admitted, accepting that there was no way to keep that information from her friend.

"The man moves even faster than I remembered."

"It's not a date," Zoe told her.

"According to whom?"

"Both of us."

"You discussed the fact that you were having dinner together and agreed that it wasn't a date?"

She nodded.

Her friend chuckled. "One of you was lying."

"It's a business meeting, to discuss ideas for renovating my house."

"Uh-huh. And where is this...business meeting... taking place?"

Zoe sighed. "At Mason's."

"Uh-huh," Claire said again, her eyes twinkling.

"You're making a big deal out of something that really isn't."

"Maybe we should wait until tomorrow to discuss which one of us doesn't have a clear picture of what this business-meeting-at-Mason's-house really means."

"Now I'm definitely going to cancel."

"Don't," her friend said quickly. "Please. Give him a chance. Give *yourself* a chance."

Zoe shook her head. "I'm not ready."

Claire laid a gentle hand on her arm. "I don't mean to push. And you shouldn't let yourself be pushed if you're really not ready. But I worry that you're using everything that's happened in the past year-and-a-half as an excuse to put your life on hold. You need to start living again."

"I want to," she admitted softly. "But I'm scared. Not of Mason, but of the way I feel when I'm around him."

"Which means that you're feeling something," her friend pointed out smugly.

It had been a long time since she'd felt anything other than disappointment and despair, sorrow and regret. When she'd found Hadfield House, she felt the first stirrings of hope and joy and excitement and anticipation. And then she'd met Mason, and suddenly she was feeling all kinds of things she wasn't prepared for.

"Lust," she admitted on a wistful sigh. "Pure unadulterated lust."

Claire's smile came back in full force. "A very good sign."

Zoe shook her head. "Except that my sexual experience is extremely limited, and although my hormones are showing definite signs of life again, my heart isn't ready. I can't face that kind of rejection again."

"I'm not suggesting you fall in love with the man. Just spend some time with him, see where things go."

"They might not go anywhere," Zoe said.

"You never know." Her friend's smile turned to a frown when her watch beeped. "I didn't realize what time it was getting to be. I have to run or I'll be late getting Laurel to gymnastics."

Zoe followed her to the door. "Thanks—for the housewarming gifts and especially for all of your help. The house looks a thousand times better already."

"I think we made enough progress that you won't

need to feel guilty about taking a few hours for your dinner-with-Mason-that-isn't-a-date."

"It isn't a date," Zoe said again.

"Of course not."

Her eyes narrowed in suspicion of her friend's easy agreement.

"Just one last piece of advice before I go," Claire said.

"What's that?"

"Take the chardonnay."

After Claire had gone, Zoe continued to work. But with every minute that passed, bringing her another minute closer to her scheduled dinner meeting with Mason, her trepidation grew.

Last night she hadn't thought twice about marching over there, propelled by anger and indignation that his dog had been trespassing again. Tonight, she was an invited guest, and for some inexplicable reason, that left her a jumble of tangled nerves.

It's just dinner, she reminded herself. It wasn't a date—Mason had said so himself.

So why was she so nervous just thinking about it?

Why did she feel as if she would be crossing some kind of line she wasn't ready to cross?

She tried to find reassurance in Mason's assertion that he didn't date married women. Except that he knew she was just waiting for her divorce to be final, and she wondered if he was waiting, too.

It didn't seem to occur to him that the interest he'd expressed might not be reciprocated. Probably because he was built like a statue of a god and had a smile that would melt any woman's reservations at ten paces. As it might have melted hers had her personal circumstances been different.

But the truth was, she had a lot of things to work out on her own before she considered getting involved with anyone again. She'd meant it when she'd told him she wasn't ready to start dating, and she wasn't going to change her mind because a simple look from Mason Sullivan made her heart race. Her heart was still too battered and bruised from everything she'd been through over the past year-and-a-half to want to open it up again.

Even before she had met her husband, she hadn't been the type to engage in casual relationships. She'd had very definite plans for her life that didn't leave much time for meaningless flirtations or recreational sex. She'd wanted a home and a family—but mostly she'd wanted the stability she hadn't had growing up.

She'd thought she was getting everything she wanted when she had married Scott, that her dreams were finally within her grasp. And for the first few years of their marriage, she had continued to believe it. They'd discussed their plans for a family, talked excitedly about having a baby, and Zoe had believed he'd wanted a child as much as she had. But whenever she'd pressed, he had balked. *Maybe next year.* Except that next year had never come.

She'd finally gone in for a checkup, wanting her doctor's okay before she brought up the subject again. But the doctor hadn't given her the okay. Instead, he'd scheduled a follow-up exam, which had led to additional tests, and somewhere along the way Zoe had started wanting the normalcy of her life back even more than she wanted a baby.

She'd heard people say it about other couples who had separated—well, at least they didn't have children. As if that was supposed to be some sort of consolation. She knew the same thing had been said when her marriage had fallen apart, but Zoe wasn't grateful for the fact. More than anything, she'd wanted a baby, a family, a home. And now, only months away from her thirtieth birthday, she was painfully aware of being alone.

When she and Scott had exchanged vows, she'd thought that was something she would never have to worry about again. Now that their divorce was almost final, she realized she'd been alone for a lot longer than the period of their separation. They'd been living separate lives under the same roof without even realizing it, until that roof had caved in and the foundation of everything had crumbled.

Her husband was the first man she'd ever loved, the only man she'd thought she would ever love, and it had broken her heart to acknowledge the end of their marriage. When she'd packed up her belongings and walked out of their apartment for the last time, she couldn't have imagined ever wanting to get involved in a relationship that would risk her heart again.

Yet despite all that painful history, she couldn't deny that she was attracted to her new neighbor, and that was what unnerved her the most. It was easy enough to discount what he said or did—obviously flirting came as naturally to Mason Sullivan as breathing. But what was she supposed to do about these feelings he stirred inside her?

Embrace them, Claire had said. *You've been numb for far too long.*

But Claire was stronger than she was, braver than she was.

Zoe wanted only to ignore the feelings. She wasn't ready to do anything else.

So she dropped the cloth back into the bucket of soapy water and dried her hands. Then she picked up her cell phone and called Mason to decline his dinner invitation.

She wasn't sure if she was relieved or disappointed when his voice mail clicked in after the third ring. She listened to the low, sexy voice that carried just the slightest hint of the south and wondered, as she was advised to leave a message, if it was in bad taste to cancel plans electronically. Then she decided she didn't care—it was a matter of self-preservation. Besides, it was a Saturday, and she had no doubt that Mason Sullivan wouldn't have any trouble making alternative plans for his evening. And she had enough work to do to keep busy until she fell into an exhausted—and hopefully dreamless—slumber.

Mason spent most of Saturday at the office, catching up on some work and figuring out a schedule for new projects then, when Nick had popped in, filling his partner in on the latest business developments. After Nick had gone home to his wife and new baby girl,

Mason headed to the grocery story to pick up a couple of steaks and a few other things for his dinner with Zoe.

He was whistling as he loaded up his grocery cart, looking forward to spending a few hours in the company of an interesting and attractive woman. Not a date but a dinner meeting, he reminded himself, although he wasn't convinced the distinction was anything more than semantics.

But he understood Zoe's reluctance to jump back into the dating pool before her divorce was final. There were a lot of piranhas in that pool and an unsuspecting swimmer could get eaten alive. It was natural that she would be hesitant, maybe even wary. Heck, recent experience had made *him* wary.

Until meeting Zoe had piqued his curiosity enough to make him want to test the waters again. Except the thought of getting back out there didn't entice him as much as the thought of being with her. Which might prove to be something of a dilemma since she'd been clear that she wasn't looking for any kind of personal relationship. But Mason was confident that, with a little time and some gentle persuasion, he could change her mind. In fact, it was a challenge he looked forward to.

His confidence took a serious hit when he got home from the grocery store and heard the message Zoe had left on his voice mail.

He was disappointed by the change of plans—then annoyed with himself for letting it matter enough that he could be disappointed.

He shoved the steaks into the refrigerator and

reached for the phone to call for pizza. He had no intention of sitting around and thinking about a canceled business meeting that wasn't even a date.

But he hesitated before punching in the number that he knew from memory because he really didn't want to spend yet another Saturday night sitting at home alone.

He tried calling his brother but got his machine. Then he sat and stared at the phone as he considered his other options. It was disheartening to realize how limited those options were.

He wasn't so desperate for company that he would intrude on Nick and Jessica while they were still settling in with their new baby. And though he had other friends, most of them had families or wives or at least significant others with whom they would be spending their evening.

His attention shifted when Rosie propped his chin on Mason's thigh. He ruffled the thick fur on the top of the dog's head. "Looks like it's just you and me tonight," he said. "You want pepperoni or sausage on that pizza?"

Rosie gave one short bark and went straight to the door.

"Okay—walk and then pizza."

He went to the back door, sighing when the animal streaked past him and immediately tore off through the woods toward Zoe's house.

Okay, maybe he'd suspected that Rosie would head in that direction. The dog's infatuation with their new neighbor had been immediate and enthusiastic—and obviously one-sided. And maybe, Mason mused wryly as he made his way through the woods, he and the dog had more in common than he wanted to admit.

He could hear the music before he stepped out of the

trees—Bruce Springsteen singing about "Glory Days." As he crossed the sloped lawn, the gravelly voice grew louder and was joined by another voice—this one decidedly feminine and definitely off-key. He smiled as he listened to her sing at the top of her lungs, thinking that she was trying to compensate with enthusiasm for what she lacked in talent.

He stepped onto the porch and knocked, but of course, she didn't hear the rap of his knuckles on the wood door. She probably couldn't hear anything over the pulsing beat of the music. He tried again, banging harder this time. Then gave up and tried the handle, surprised to find it unlocked.

He hesitated, because he knew she'd be annoyed if he just walked in. On the other hand, she was the one who'd left the door unlocked—which wasn't so unusual in a town like Pinehurst but unexpected of someone recently moved from the big city.

The dog had his big head halfway through the door before Mason had eased it open even a few inches.

"You have to stay here," he said.

Rosie's head tipped back, and he stared beseechingly at his owner through dark liquid eyes.

"I don't understand it, either," Mason assured him. "But for some reason, you're not her favorite animal right now, especially since you're not on an *l-e-a-s-h*, so it would be best if you just waited out here for a while."

The dog reluctantly backed out of the door and settled onto the porch, though he was clearly none too happy about being relegated to the outside.

Although he felt another tug of guilt, Mason none-theless closed the door tightly to ensure that Rosie stayed out before following the music up the stairs.

He found Zoe in one of the bedrooms on the second level.

She was on a ladder, about halfway up, and putting all the muscle she had in her slender arms into scrubbing the walls. Her hair was tied back in a loose ponytail from which several strands had escaped and were clinging damply to her neck. She was wearing a tiny little tank top that didn't quite meet the top of her cut-off shorts, and when she reached up, several inches of pale skin were exposed. Her legs were toned and tanned, her feet tucked into battered sneakers.

There was a square fan in the window, but it seemed only to circulate rather than cool the air. The portable CD player blasted out another Springsteen song. She wasn't singing along anymore, but the volume of the music still prohibited any attempt at conversation so he crossed over to the boom box and pressed the stop button.

The abrupt quiet obviously startled Zoe, because she pivoted quickly. Too quickly considering her precarious perch on the narrow step.

The ladder wobbled; she wobbled.

Mason instinctively reached up to steady her.

But as his hands caught her around the waist, his palms came into contact with the smooth warm skin of her exposed midriff.

He heard her inhale sharply, saw her eyes widen and felt the air fairly crackle around them.

The moment seemed to spin out between them, re-flected in the emotions that swirled through the depths of her dark eyes.

Surprise.

Confusion.

Awareness.

Desire.

Apparently the needs that were churning inside of him were churning inside of her, too, and wasn't that a lucky coincidence?

But along with the desire he could see in her eyes, there was wariness, too. It was the wariness that had her leaning back, away from the pull of whatever was drawing them together.

As she did, her elbow hit the bucket that was perched on the top step of the ladder.

He watched helplessly as the pail tipped forward.

Chapter Five

Zoe let out a startled squeal as the sudsy water splashed over her.

Without thinking about the fact that she was still perched on the ladder, she launched herself out of the way of the waterfall—and into Mason's arms.

He stumbled back a step but held on, gathering her against his chest so she wouldn't fall.

The shock of the surprise shower made her stiffen; the warm, solid strength of his body made her melt.

Oh my, was all she could think, as she absorbed the unexpected and thrilling sensation of being held tightly against him.

Their bodies were aligned intimately from shoulders to knees, her breasts crushed against the hard wall of his chest, her thighs trapped between his. And he was hot and hard and gloriously male everywhere she touched.

He was also, she reminded herself, her neighbor. And her heart was too fragile to risk the consequences of lusting after any man.

His arms remained locked firmly on her waist as he lowered her to the ground.

Slowly.

Inch by inch.

And with every inch, she was achingly aware of her body sliding against his, of the rising heat generated by that friction. So much heat, intense and unexpected, that she wondered that she didn't spontaneously combust.

She finally felt the floor beneath her feet, but it seemed to be shifting and tilting, keeping her off-balance. And the hands that had automatically grabbed hold of him when she'd fallen continued to grip the muscles of his arms as the world spun around her.

She exhaled a slow, unsteady breath and tried to shake off the fuzzy cloud of sensation that was fogging her brain.

She tipped her head back, to tell him that he could let her go. But the dark intensity of his gaze took her breath away, and the unspoken words tumbled silently out of her mind and into oblivion.

His lips curved in a slow, sexy smile that made her mouth go dry and her heart beat so hard against her ribs she worried that he could feel it.

"Well, this is unexpected," he said. "And very, very nice."

She wasn't sure *nice* was the word she would have

chosen. It was far too tame to describe the wild currents that were suddenly ricocheting through her system.

"I have to admit, I've wondered about this," he said huskily.

She had to moisten her lips before she could ask, "About what?"

"How you would feel in my arms."

"Oh."

"You feel good, Zoe." His hands skimmed up her back, then down again.

She tried to focus, to think of the thousand and one reasons that this shouldn't be happening, but her mind was fuzzy, and reason was a misty cloud rapidly dissipating in the heat being generated between them.

"I'm wet," was the only response she could manage.

His lightning-quick grin made her cheeks flush.

"You still feel good," he said. "Although I wouldn't object if you wanted to take off those clothes."

She managed to pull herself out of his arms, to somehow support herself on rubbery legs.

She suspected that he was the type of man who would press if he knew he had the advantage. Zoe had no intention of letting him know that those long, steady looks made her stomach muscles quiver and his slow, easy smiles turned her knees to jelly.

Eight days, she reminded herself. She'd met this man only eight days ago, and she knew that if she wasn't careful, she'd find herself in bed with him before another eight days were up.

She took a step back, away from the heat of his touch and the reach of temptation.

"I need to, uh, mop this up."

But Mason had already reached the mop that was propped against the wall. "It looks like you've made strides toward getting this place into shape already."

Zoe tugged her sodden T-shirt away from her body and squeezed some of the water out of it. "Other than the lake on the floor, you mean?"

He smiled. "Yeah, other than that."

"A friend of mine stopped by this morning to give me a hand."

"I didn't know you knew anyone in town." He dragged the mop through the puddle.

"No one except Claire. At least, not until I bought this place. Now people seem to be coming out of the woodwork.

"I met Harry Anderson at the hardware store yesterday, had lunch with my real estate agent, and today Doug Metler—the local mailman—knocked on the door to say 'hi.'"

"I know who Doug is."

"I should have figured you would. But I've never known the name of any of my mail carriers before. Anyway, after Doug went on his way, Tess Richmond from across the street came over to welcome me to the neighborhood, and Ron Griffiths from down the street brought over some blueberry muffins that his wife had baked."

"Irene makes great muffins, doesn't she?"

She blew out a breath as she reached for the mop to finish the cleanup, but he shook his head and continued to soak up the spill.

"Yes, they were great muffins," she said. "But that's hardly the point."

His smile widened. "I warned you that you'd find living in Pinehurst quite an adjustment after the big city. And though most people are genuinely friendly and helpful, you will meet some who are just plain nosy."

"I'm still trying to figure out which category you fit into," she admitted.

"I would think the fact that I'm holding a mop should answer that question."

"Maybe. But you still haven't told me why you're really here, and, as much as I appreciate the effort, I don't think it's to wash my floors."

"You're right," he admitted. "I came over to take another look at the attic, talk about the renovations and find out how you like your pizza."

"It's Saturday night," she reminded him. "Don't you have anything better to do?"

"I did have plans," he said. "But my date called at the eleventh hour to cancel. Left a message on my voice mail, if you can believe that."

"It wasn't the eleventh hour," she said. "It was several hours before the scheduled meeting time that you said *wasn't* a date."

He shrugged. "Whether it was or not, you still bailed on me."

She had, and because she still felt a little guilty about that, she couldn't meet his gaze when she said, "Because I have too much to do around here."

"Yeah, I can see why you wouldn't want to take a break for something as trivial as a meal."

"I took a break for lunch."

"What time was that?" he challenged.

"I don't know." But the low rumble in her stomach betrayed the fact that it had been several hours before.

And Mason's quick grin told her that the sound had not gone unnoticed. "So what do you like on your pizza?"

She sighed. "Just cheese."

He finished mopping up the spill and put the mop inside the bucket. "Not very adventurous, are you?"

"Is there something wrong with enjoying the simple things in life?"

"Not at all." He smiled. "Just as there's nothing wrong with a little variety—or spicing things up every once in a while."

She was no longer certain they were talking about pizza, so she remained silent.

"Why don't I order while you're changing your clothes?"

"I never said I wanted pizza."

"No, but your stomach did."

She couldn't argue with that. Instead she said, "My cell phone's on the table in the dining room."

Mason was just hanging up the phone when Zoe came down the stairs.

She was wearing a pair of well-worn jeans and an oversized T-shirt now, but her feet were bare and her hair had been brushed out of its ponytail and hung loose to her shoulders.

"I liked the shorts better," he told her.

"The shorts are now in a rapidly growing pile of dirty laundry," she told him.

"At least you can't blame Rosie for *this* wardrobe mishap."

"No," she agreed, then narrowed her eyes. "But speaking of the beast, where is he?"

"On your porch."

"You left him outside?" she asked incredulously. "Alone?"

"I didn't figure you wanted dog hair all over the house you've been working so hard to get clean."

"I don't," she agreed. "But you can't just leave him alone outside. What if he ran away? Or somebody tried to take him?"

He chuckled at that. "The only place Rosie has ever run is here. And can you imagine anyone wanting to steal that animal?"

"Probably not," she admitted, her mouth turning up at the corners. "But maybe you should let him in, anyway, so he doesn't scare off the pizza delivery boy."

"Are you sure?"

"I don't dislike your dog," she said, moving into the kitchen. "I just don't like his habit of pouncing on me from out of nowhere."

Mason opened the front door, grabbing hold of Rosie's collar before he went tearing through the house in search of Zoe. "Down," he said, then released his hold.

Rosie didn't jump, but his whole body quivered with the effort of restraining himself. And when he reached Zoe's side, he rubbed his head affectionately against her thigh, leaving a smear of white dog hair on her jeans.

Zoe sighed as she patted his head. "You really are a beast."

The dog just stared at her adoringly.

She shook her head and turned her attention to Mason. "Can I get you something to drink?"

"What have you got?"

She scanned the contents of her refrigerator. "7UP, orange juice, water and white wine."

"Red wine goes better with pizza," he told her.

"Well, white is all I've got. Do you want a glass or not?"

"Sure."

She dug through a box of unpacked utensils on the counter until she found a corkscrew, then adeptly uncorked the bottle and poured wine into two juice glasses.

"I haven't got around to washing any of the stemware yet," she explained, handing him one of the glasses.

"I remember chugging back wine from the bottle on one or two occasions when I was in college," he said. "This is definitely a step up."

Her lips curved, and he was struck again by how truly beautiful she was when she smiled.

"To clean floors," she said, holding up her drink.

"And to pizza in thirty minutes or less," he added, touching the rim of his glass to hers.

Rosie barked, clearly insulted that he'd been left out of the toast.

Zoe looked down at him. "Are you thirsty, too?"

She took a bottle of water from the fridge and emptied it into a bowl for the dog.

Rosie barked again, in appreciation this time, and immediately began slurping.

"Tap water would have been fine," Mason told her.

"The tap water still looks a little rusty—I don't even like to shower in it, never mind drink it."

"Rosie wouldn't care. He'll drink out of the toilet if I forget to put the lid down."

She shuddered at the thought as she pulled out the stool on the opposite side of the breakfast bar and sat down across from him.

"What's with the camera?" he asked.

She froze with her glass halfway to her lips, her eyes sliding across the counter to the item in question as if she'd never seen it before. "Oh. That. It's, um, Claire's. She thought I should take pictures of the house to document the work in progress."

"That's a good idea," he agreed. "Though I would have expected a photographer would have her own camera."

She took a long swallow of her drink. "I have several, but I put all of my equipment in storage when—before—I moved."

Before he could press, the doorbell rang. Rosie raced for the front door, barking and dancing in circles on the way.

"Must be the pizza," he said. "He goes nuts for pizza."

"I think he's just nuts—period," Zoe muttered as she pushed back her chair. "Can you get the door while I run up to get some money?"

Mason started to tell her that he'd put the order on his account, but she was already halfway up the stairs.

He shrugged and went to answer the door.

And found it wasn't the usual delivery kid but a gorgeous—and familiar—woman standing on the porch.

"Claire?"

The surprise that flashed in her eyes turned to pleasure, and the quick and easy smile that curved her lips took him back fifteen years. "Hello, Mason."

"You're Zoe's friend," he suddenly realized.

She nodded. "Is she here?"

"Yeah. Uh, come in." He stood back so that she could enter. "I didn't realize—she mentioned a friend named Claire, but I never suspected it might be Claire Kennedy."

"It's been Lamontagne for eleven years now," she told him.

Before he could say anything else, the doorbell rang again and Zoe was coming back down the stairs.

"*That* will be the delivery boy," Mason said, as Rosie started dancing and barking again.

"Do you want to stay for a slice of pizza?" he heard Zoe ask Claire when he turned around with the box in hand.

"No, thanks. Rob and the kids are waiting in the car. We're on our way out to a movie, but when I saw the lights on here, I thought you might have cancelled your—" she paused to smile "—date, and I was going to ask you to join us."

"Mason just stopped by to discuss the renovations," Zoe said.

"Because you did cancel our date," he felt compelled to add.

Claire smiled again as she sent her friend a look as if to say "I told you so."

"Have fun at the movies," Zoe said to Claire. Then to Mason, "I'll go get plates and napkins."

His eyes followed her progress across the floor, enjoying the gentle sway of her hips as she disappeared into the kitchen. When he turned his attention back to Claire, he saw her gaze narrowed on him, considering.

"Are you going to ask me to stay away from your friend?"

"No. Partly because Zoe wouldn't appreciate my interference, and partly because I think you could be good for her."

"So much for my reputation as the type of guy mothers warn their daughters about."

Claire smiled. "Your reputation is still intact," she assured him. "Believe me, I am a mother, though I hope I won't have to be warning my daughter about men like you for a lot of years yet. But I'm also a woman, so I can appreciate that a woman sometimes needs a man her mother wouldn't approve of."

"Thank you, I think."

She chuckled. "I won't ask you to stay away from Zoe, but I will ask you to be careful, though."

"I'm not in the habit of being anything else," he told her.

Claire hesitated, as if she wanted to say more, but then she only nodded as she reached for the door. "Enjoy your pizza."

Zoe took the plates and wine into the dining room. It was less cluttered than the kitchen, she reasoned, and wasn't at all motivated by her curiosity to know what

Claire and Mason were discussing. Which was just as well, since she couldn't hear them, anyway.

It had surprised her to learn that her friend had dated the architect. Maybe because she knew how happy Claire was in her marriage, and Rob—although truly a fabulous man who was devoted to his wife—had nothing on Mason Sullivan. But what did she know? She was basing her assumptions on the contrast of her warm, cordial feelings toward Rob and the hot jolt of awareness that zinged through her system whenever she was near Mason.

And when she thought about it, she realized that although her friend was privy to all of her deepest secrets, she really hadn't known Claire for very long. Not even two years—though those years sometimes felt like a lifetime.

As she settled into a chair to wait for Mason to bring in the pizza, her mind drifted back to the day she had met Claire.

It was a day that had irrevocably changed the direction of her life, setting her on the path that had brought her to the time and place she was at right now.

She remembered that Scott had offered to go with her to the hospital the day of her mastectomy. Just as she remembered thinking, even then, that he'd made the offer as a courtesy rather than out of any real desire to be with her. Instead, she'd taken a taxi, insisting that she wanted to be alone. She'd checked in, then changed into her surgical gown, climbed onto the gurney and prepared to wait and battle alone against the panic escalating inside of her.

Then Claire had walked in.

Prior to that day, Zoe had communicated with her only via e-mail and, less frequently, by telephone. She'd never seen her before, would never have guessed who she was until she'd said, *Hi, Zoe. I'm Claire.*

And for some inexplicable reason, Zoe's eyes had filled with tears and her throat had tightened. She wanted to ask why the other woman was there, but she suddenly hadn't been able to speak and knew that if she tried, she'd fall apart.

Claire, unfazed by Zoe's silence, had sat down beside the bed and taken her hand. *I'm here for you. Because I've been where you are, and no one should ever have to go through this alone.*

She'd stayed when they'd taken Zoe down to surgery and was waiting in the same spot when they'd brought her back up again.

She was the one person Zoe had truly felt she could count on, the one person who had been there for her when no one else had been, the one person who had really seemed to know who she was and what she'd wanted.

Which brought her full circle back to the question: Did she want Mason Sullivan?

I'm not suggesting you fall in love with him. Claire's voice echoed in the back of her mind. *Just spend some time with him, see where things go.*

When Mason walked into the room, she felt that hot jolt again and decided that she just might follow her friend's advice after all.

It wasn't quite how Mason had planned to spend his Saturday night, but he couldn't complain about the fact that he was seated across from a beautiful and intriguing woman, sharing a bottle of good wine and a Marco's extra-large. Candlelight and soft music might have added some ambience, but he thought it just as likely such overtly romantic touches would make Zoe even more wary.

He wasn't a patient man by nature. If given the choice, he would always choose instant gratification over long-term gains. He preferred the rush of playing the stock market to the security of government bonds. On the other hand, he had a clear understanding of the differences between a woman and a financial investment, and he appreciated that a more cautious approach sometimes reaped greater rewards.

He knew he would need to be very cautious with Zoe. He was equally certain the rewards would make it worthwhile.

As he transferred a slice of pizza to his plate, he thought they were off to a pretty good start. A casual meal and some light conversation should help her warm up to him a little.

The bump against his thigh had him tacking an addendum onto that thought: so long as Rosie didn't blow it for him. Again.

"This is good," Zoe said.

"It's even better with sausage," he told her, discreetly sneaking a piece of crust under the table to Rosie.

"I'll take your word for it."

"You really don't like sausage on pizza?"

"No."

"Pepperoni?"

"I really like just cheese."

"What's your favorite color?"

She licked a smear of pizza sauce from her thumb and frowned at the unexpected question. "I don't have one."

"Favorite baseball team?"

"I don't watch baseball."

"Basketball?"

She shook her head.

"Football? Soccer? Hockey?"

"None of the above."

"Okay—who's your favorite Stooge?"

"*The Three Stooges* are the only thing more tedious than professional sports."

He frowned and nibbled on a piece of sausage.

"James Bond?" he asked cautiously.

Her lips curved. "Sean Connery."

"Favorite movie?"

"Why all the questions?"

"I'm curious about you." He picked up the bottle of wine, topped up both of their glasses. "And all I've managed to learn through observation and inference is that you like cheese pizza, Australian wine, and you sing along with the radio—or at least with Springsteen."

She paused with her glass halfway to her lips. "You heard that?"

He grinned. "I'll never be able to listen to The Boss again without thinking of you."

"I'll never be able to sing 'Glory Days' again

without remembering the humiliation of this moment."

He decided not to state the obvious—that she really wasn't able to sing it before.

"Now you have to share something you've done that is just as embarrassing," she told him.

He grinned. "I've never done anything *that* embarrassing."

At her narrowed stare, he chuckled.

"And why am I supposed to tell you a story that reveals my humiliation?"

"So that I won't have to move out of the neighborhood to maintain my dignity."

"Alright," he relented. "In second grade I insisted on wearing my Batman pajamas to school."

She just stared across the table at him, waiting.

"Every day for a whole week," he continued.

The roll of her eyes suggested that she still wasn't impressed.

"Because I thought I really was Batman."

Her gaze narrowed. "Really?"

He shrugged. "I was seven and had a vivid imagination."

"Okay, that might have been embarrassing," she allowed. "But I was thinking about something that might have happened in the past decade or so."

"Well, my most recent source of embarrassment would have to be my dog, who suddenly seems to have developed an obsession with my new neighbor."

"An obsession?"

He nodded. "She only moved in about a week ago,

but every time I turn around, he's escaping from my backyard to visit her—and usually wreaking some kind of havoc in the process."

"Are you afraid that she'll call animal control?"

"Nah. I'm more worried that she won't look past the menace that my dog has become to see what a great guy I am."

"Why does that worry you?"

"Because I like her."

Her brow furrowed as she lifted a second slice of pizza from the box. "If she only moved in a week ago, you can't know her very well."

"Yeah, but I'm working on that."

She took her time wiping her fingers with a paper napkin. "You might find, once you get to know her, that you don't really like her after all."

"What worries you, Zoe—that I won't? or that I will?"

She lifted her head to meet his gaze. "You don't worry me."

Oh, yes, I do, he thought, pleased to realize that he did. Pleased to know that he could shake her cool confidence with just a word, a look, a touch. And curious about how she would respond when he really did touch her.

"Then tell me," he said, "what made you wake up one morning and decide you wanted to stop taking pictures and start making pancakes instead?"

"Actually, a bed-and-breakfast never even occurred to me until the real estate agent mentioned the possibility. I just wanted the house."

"And you took the idea and ran with it?"

She shrugged. "Seemed like a good idea."

There was still something she wasn't telling him. He didn't know why he was so certain, only that he was.

"Well, I was able to get copies of the original blueprints for the house," he told her. "Which makes my job a lot easier. I should have the plans for your renovations drafted by the end of next week, so you can start looking for a contractor to oversee the work."

"You said you would give me some names," she reminded him.

He nodded. "There are several companies in town that do good work. Barclay Builders, Carson Construction, Pinehurst Rehab & Renovation."

"Who would you recommend?"

"Any of those would—"

"If you needed work done," she interrupted. "Who would you call?"

"Pinehurst Rehab. But that might be because it's my brother's company."

"If I mention your name, will he cut me a deal—or double his rates?"

Mason laughed. "Hard to say, although I'd guess on the deal because he has a soft spot for pretty women."

"Something that runs in the family?"

"Wherever would you get that idea?"

"Claire," she told him. "She warned me about you."

"What did she say?" he asked, more curious than insulted.

"That you'd probably hit on me before you finished drawing up the plans for my renovations."

"Well, proper planning takes time. And a beautiful

woman is hard to resist." He emptied what was left of the wine into her glass. "Even when that beautiful woman is technically still married to someone else."

"Are you hitting on me?"

"I don't hit on married women." But he reached over to tuck a strand of hair behind her ear, smiled when she went still. "Usually."

Her eyes darkened, her breath caught, confirming his suspicion that she wasn't as unaffected as she pretended to be. He let his fingertips trail down her throat, felt the flutter of her pulse and wondered how she would react if he pressed his lips there. The wondering made him want; the wanting made him worry.

He dropped his hand and sat back.

"I should go," he said. "Before I forget that there are rules to the game."

"I was married for nine years," she reminded him. "I don't even know the game, never mind how to play it."

His gaze locked with hers, held. "Are you trying to warn me or tempt me?"

"I'm trying to be honest. I'm not looking for a relationship or a fling or anything in between."

"Then I'll be honest, too," he said, "and tell you that I'm going to do my darnedest to change your mind."

Chapter Six

It took Zoe a full two weeks to get the house thoroughly cleaned, and when that was done, she turned her attention to the jungle that had taken over the yard outside. She considered hiring a landscaper to get rid of the weeds and cut back everything that had grown wild over the past couple of years, but although she'd never been much of a gardener, it somehow seemed like cheating. This was her rehab project, and although she knew she couldn't handle every aspect of it on her own, she wanted to make the effort to do as much as she could.

Claire was a lot more knowledgeable than she was about flowers and stuff, and she'd promised that the beds would fill with colorful blooms if she got rid of the weeds that were choking the flowers. Zoe was making a valiant effort while keeping her fingers crossed that she was actually pulling out the weeds and not the flowers.

On her second day in the garden, Zoe was tackling the perimeter on the east side of the property when she heard an unfamiliar chirping sound. Not that she was yet able to identify any of the birdsongs that normally serenaded her in the morning, but there was something about this impatient, almost frantic, peeping sound that urged her to leave her trowel in the dirt and explore.

As she made her way toward a trio of evergreen trees, the sound grew louder. She knelt on the damp ground and carefully lifted the low-lying branches of the widest tree. There was a nest on the ground, and she immediately feared that it had fallen. But on closer inspection, she saw that it was upright and intact and the baby birds inside appeared unharmed. Noisy—but unharmed.

She shuffled a little closer for a better view. There were four babies, recently hatched, she figured, as they were still mostly bald with their eyes closed and their open beaks thrust into the air.

She was so awed by the discovery that she didn't stop to think but hurried into the house for the camera that Claire had left when she came to visit that first time. She was on her belly on the ground, propped up on her elbows and snapping pictures when a louder, more frantic call drew her gaze to the sky.

The mother bird, she guessed, as it swooped toward her, screaming and flapping. Zoe didn't know if the bird would really attack, but she wasn't taking any chances. She made a quick retreat, the camera clutched tightly in her hand.

She kept her distance after that, using the zoom function to capture images of the mother ducking under the cover of the tree to feed her babies, then backing out again to hunt down more food. She didn't know how long she'd been watching when she heard the sharp, familiar bark then saw Rosie tearing across the lawn. The beast was making a beeline for her when it fell into the mother bird's radar. Obviously concerned for her babies, she dove toward Rosie.

Zoe held her breath, worried that the dog might somehow get hold of the mother, then let it out on a laugh when Rosie cowered in response to the bird's cries. When the bird flew away again, Rosie jumped up, dancing around and barking like a lunatic. Zoe lifted the camera again, snapping pictures until she'd finished off the first roll of film and was well into another.

The strange bird-dog dance ended only when Rosie was distracted by another of his favorite people—the mailman. Zoe scrambled to her feet to rescue him from Rosie's slobbering affection.

Thankfully, Doug didn't appear to be annoyed or intimidated by the beast.

"Looks like you're settling in and making friends with the neighbors," he commented.

"Yeah, I can see how it would look like that."

He grinned at her dry tone as he passed her a handful of letters. "I've got mail for Mason, too. Do you want me to take Rosie back?"

"No, it's alright. He'll wander back on his own when I go inside."

"Alright then." Doug lifted his hand in a wave as he headed back down the long gravel drive. "Have a good day."

"You, too," she said, smiling over the brief conversation with her mailman.

The smile faded when she flipped through her mail and saw the seal on the corner of the largest envelope. She carried it to the step and sat down, lifting the flap with trembling fingers.

In the Petition for Divorce that had been filed with the court, she was listed as petitioner and Scott Cowan was the respondent. While they'd both agreed that there were irreconcilable differences, Zoe was the one who'd wanted to formalize the break—she needed to clean the slate in order to start her life over again.

So it was ridiculous to experience a jolt of surprise when she opened that envelope and found her decree of divorce, signed by the judge and stamped by the court. It was just an official document confirming the legal fact of what she'd known for months—her marriage was over.

But she was surprised, and she was saddened to know that a union forged with so much pomp and circumstance could conclude with a routine mail delivery. That the hopes and dreams she and Scott had taken with them into their marriage had somehow been lost in their journey together.

Zoe tucked the decree back into the envelope, shoving the memories and regrets alongside it.

* * *

Mason wasn't sure what it was about Zoe that had gotten under his skin, but he found himself thinking about her at the oddest times during the day—and dreaming about her at night. No other woman had intruded on his thoughts the way she seemed to do, and that realization baffled as much as it annoyed him.

He wasn't entirely sure what it was about her that appealed to him. She was closer to skinny than slender and might have been described as having a boyish figure if not for the subtle swell of her breasts and the gentle curve of her hips. And yet, despite his usual preference for curvier women, he found that willow build alluring.

But it was the eyes, he decided, that really drew him in. There was something about those dark fathomless depths that seemed to reflect so much of what she was feeling and still hint at secrets. Or maybe it was her mouth—with its delicate shape and lush lips that were quick to curve. Or the soft, throaty laugh that sometimes spilled out so unexpectedly and never failed to punch him in the gut.

Not since his crush on Holly James in seventh grade had Mason allowed himself to be so distracted by a woman.

He'd had relationships, of course. Some people would say more than his fair share. But Mason approached dating the same way he approached fishing— for the sheer pleasure of it and never with the intention of hanging on to anything he caught. Not for very long, anyway, he thought with a grin.

But he made sure that the women he dated enjoyed the experience as much as he did. He was always honest about what he wanted—a good time—and clear about what he didn't—anything even remotely hinting at a commitment. If a lover was shocked when their involvement ended, it was because she obviously hadn't been paying attention to what he'd been saying.

There had, admittedly, been a few of those over the years. And more than usual in recent experience. It was as if there was something in the genetic makeup of women that allowed them to believe a twenty-five- or thirty-year-old guy just wanted a good time, but as soon as he passed the threshold of his thirty-fifth birthday, they assumed he was looking for the right woman to settle down with despite all assurances to the contrary. And when he finally managed to convince a woman that he did *not* want to live together or get married or whatever else she was set on, she stormed out, as if he'd misled her all along.

Maybe that was why he liked Zoe. He figured a woman just emerging from one failed marriage wouldn't be looking to jump into another one again.

But whatever the reasons for his attraction to his new neighbor, he genuinely enjoyed spending time with her. And he'd found frequent occasions and excuses to do so, even if it was only a half hour conversation in her backyard during one of his habitual walks with Rosie. Though Zoe still eyed the dog with wariness and trepidation, she'd stopped threatening to buy rope so that he could tie the animal up. In fact, when she'd told him about Rosie and the birds, she'd sounded amused

108 THE NEW GIRL IN TOWN

rather than annoyed by the dog's antics. He liked to think that she was warming up to him as well as his pet, and he was fairly certain the sparks of attraction were zinging in both directions when they were together.

But aside from the attraction, she was easy to be with and interesting to talk to. She had her own opinions about things and didn't seem to care if those opinions butted up against his own—as they frequently did. She had some good ideas for her house, if not the slightest clue as to the work that would be required to implement them.

She wanted the interior of the house to reflect the exterior and had thrown herself into researching the Victorian era, studying color schemes and wall coverings and window treatments from the period. She was tackling the rehab with a focused intensity and enthusiasm he couldn't help but admire even as he wondered why it seemed to take precedence over everything else—and how long she could continue before she burned herself out.

Not his problem, he reminded himself, and whistled for Rosie so they could take their afternoon walk.

But as he tromped through the woods behind the dog, he found himself wondering again about Zoe's reasons for coming to Pinehurst. He knew about restlessness and could believe it was discontent that made her leave Manhattan in search of something different. And he understood the lure of history and the hope that had persuaded her to embark on her renovation project. But he couldn't help wondering what would happen, where she would go, when it was done.

Though he was content in the town that had been his home for more than a dozen years, he knew it was a world away from New York City. A lot of people moved from smaller towns to larger cities, looking for something bigger and better. It was less common for big-city dwellers to abandon the bright lights for quiet nights.

Jessica had, he suddenly remembered. Though she hadn't abandoned her career so much as shifted both her location and focus. Besides, she'd grown up in Pinehurst—and she'd been in love with Nick forever.

That they shared a deep and powerful bond was obvious to anyone after even only a few minutes in their company. It was apparent in the way their eyes would meet and hold, even from opposite sides of a crowded room. In the way Nick touched her, frequently, casually, easily. And in the way she smiled at him, as if there wasn't anyone else in the world.

He was genuinely happy for his friends, even if he'd never wanted what they had together.

At least, he'd never wanted it before. But lately, well, he'd found himself looking at Nick, seeing the contentment on his face, his excitement over the new baby, and wondering if it was so impossible to believe that he could someday meet a woman with whom he might want to share a future—or if he already had.

Even with that disquieting thought echoing in his mind, he could hear the music pumping out through the open windows before he followed Rosie out of the woods.

It was hip-hop now, and it made him smile.

Her taste in music was like so many other things

about her—unexpected and unpredictable. And just part of what intrigued him.

The door was unlocked again, and he found her in the smallest bedroom on the second level. He walked in just as she hefted a sledgehammer off the ground and, with obvious effort, swung it at the wall. The heavy tool punched into the plaster—and stayed there. With a wriggle of her hips and a groan of frustration, she struggled to pull it out again.

"What the hell—"

Of course, she couldn't hear the roar of his voice over the blare of the music.

Clamping down on his fury, he twisted the volume control to a more reasonable level. This time, when he spoke, his voice was quiet and carefully controlled.

"What do you think you're doing with that?"

She turned, still gripping the handle of the hammer with one hand as she brushed her bangs away from her face with the back of the other. "What does it look like I'm doing?"

"It looks like you're trying to kill yourself," he said, removing the sledgehammer from her grip. "Christ, this thing almost weighs as much as you do."

She shot him a look of annoyance. "Hardly."

"Pretty close, I'd wager."

"Wager elsewhere," she suggested. "I'm busy here."

"Not with this," he told her.

She folded her arms over her chest and huffed out a breath. "You were the one who said this wall needed to come down."

"And you said you would call my brother about taking it down."

"I did. His secretary said he was tied up on another job this week, and I didn't see the point in paying someone else to do what I'm perfectly capable of doing myself," she told him.

"Are you?" he challenged.

"I'm doing it, aren't I?"

He looked at the pitiful hole in the wall. "How long have you been at it? Are your arms screaming in pain yet? Are your shoulders burning? Because they will," he promised her. "You'll break down long before that wall."

She tilted her chin. "I'm a lot tougher than I look."

"I don't doubt that for a minute, honey. But you're not cut out for this kind of physical labor."

"I can do it," she insisted.

"Why?" he asked gently.

"Because it needs to come down and—"

He cut off her explanation with a shake of his head. "Not the wall—the whole house. Whatever possessed you to want to tackle such an enormous project on your own?"

Zoe couldn't tell him the truth—he already thought she was crazy for buying this place. And suggesting that she felt some kind of kinship to this broken and damaged old home, well, even she thought that was a little crazy.

Instead, she sank down onto the edge of the bed she'd covered with old sheets to protect it from dust and debris and considered her response to his question. "Let's just say I was at a crossroads in my life."

He leaned against the dresser, facing her. "Because of the divorce?"

"Among other things."

"What other things?"

"Nosy neighbors," she said. "Now will you please let me get back to work?"

He appeared unfazed by her flippant remark but when she reached for the sledgehammer, he held it away from her.

"Find something else to do."

She blew out a breath. "I appreciate your concern, but—"

"No, you don't. You wish I'd go away and stop interfering in your life."

Her lips curved reluctantly. "That, too."

"Well, it's not going to happen. Not today, anyway." He nodded toward the doorway. "Why don't you go empty out the kitchen cupboards or something?"

The dismissal stung her pride, had her chin lifting. "I think you're forgetting that this is my house."

"Not for a minute." He sent her one of those slow, lazy grins that made everything inside her melt. "I would never have been crazy enough to sink my life savings into buying it."

"And yet, you seem to be here, at every possible opportunity, wanting to put your hands all over it," she retorted, wondering how her blood could pulse with want even when he irritated her—as he frequently seemed to do.

"You should have realized by now that the house isn't all that I want to put my hands on," he said.

She took an instinctive step back, her cheeks flooding with heat as the implication of his words finally sank in.

"Does that really come as a surprise?"

"Yes. No. I don't know."

He grinned at her again. "Just something for you to think about."

She shook her head. "I can't."

"Can't think?"

"I certainly can't think about getting involved with anyone right now. I'm not ready—"

He took a step toward her, pressed a finger against her lips, halting the flow of words. It was a gentle touch, the contact fleeting, yet her skin tingled, burned.

"You've already been thinking about it," he said.

She opened her mouth to deny it, closed it again without saying a word.

"I've been thinking about it, too," he admitted. "A lot."

"I can't—it's not—" She swallowed, a difficult task when her throat was suddenly bone dry.

That cocky grin flashed again. "You can. It is. And you will stutter a lot more before we're done."

Retreat, she decided, was less humiliating than stuttering again.

She turned to leave the room, conscious of his eyes watching her every step.

Zoe emptied out the cupboards. Not because Mason had deigned to delegate the task to her, but because it was a job that needed to be done.

If she had the money, she'd rip out everything and

rebuild the kitchen from scratch. Since she was keeping a close eye on her budget to ensure she didn't deplete her funds before all the work was done, she'd opted to refinish the cabinets instead of replace them. Fresh paint and new hardware would give the tired wood a much needed facelift.

The countertop, however, needed to go. It was the ugliest faux marble surface she'd ever seen, and chipped and stained on top of that. Granite, although pricey, would give her the solid durable surface she wanted.

The vinyl floor was yellowed with age and coming apart at the seams, and though she'd considered other options, she really wanted natural wood. She'd been thrilled to find a local supplier who was willing to give her a deal on reclaimed pine. She'd also found a rack to put over the island and she could already picture it there with copper pots hanging down.

She was so caught up in her vision of the kitchen that she forgot to stay angry with Mason for kicking her out of the upstairs bedroom that would become a second guest bathroom.

In fact, not only was she no longer angry, she was touched by his concern. Not that she needed anyone to look out for her, and ordinarily she wouldn't appreciate anyone trying to tell her what to do, but just this once, it was nice to think he cared enough to worry about her.

Scott hadn't worried about her, that was for certain. He'd had too many responsibilities at the magazine to be concerned about what she was doing. And she'd been too strong and independent to let it bother her. In fact, she probably hadn't even been aware of it—until the phone call had come from her doctor's office and she'd desperately wanted not to have to face it alone.

Well, she wasn't alone right now—as the noise emanating from upstairs reminded her. It sounded like Mason was making more progress than she had, and though she hadn't asked for his help, she was grateful for it.

She folded the top of the box she'd finished packing and pushed it aside. Then she poured a tall glass of lemonade and carried it up the stairs, curious to see how he was doing. When she got to the bedroom where he was working, she stopped in her tracks.

There was a huge hole where the wall had been, but that wasn't what caught her attention.

No—her gaze was focused on the man prying away chunks of plaster with a crowbar. He'd taken off his sweatshirt, leaving him in only a T-shirt that was damp with sweat and clinging to muscles that rippled with his every movement. Her mouth actually watered as she watched him work, noting the bunch and flex of tight muscles in his arms, his shoulders, his back.

Oh, my.

She could only stare, breathless and weak, her heart pounding, her hormones clamoring.

She wasn't sure how long she stood there, just watching and—oh, yes—wanting, before he turned his head and saw her.

"I, uh, thought you might be thirsty."

She somehow managed to make her legs move so she could carry the glass across the room to him.

"I am." He let the crowbar dangle from one hand as he reached for the drink with the other. "Thanks."

She watched his throat work as he drained the glass and felt her own go dry. His skin was slick with perspiration, and his jaw was dark with stubble. He didn't look like a man who designed houses right now, but one who built them. A man, she would bet, who was as knowledgeable and skilled about pleasuring a woman as he was drawing up a plan or tearing down a wall.

"You seem to be, uh, making good progress."

"It's coming along," he agreed. "I worked in construction through high school and college, but I forgot how much I enjoyed it."

"Well, then, I'm glad I could help you rediscover the pleasure."

"It shouldn't take me too long to finish up in here," he said. "Then we could rediscover other pleasures."

"As tempting as that sounds…no."

Mason couldn't help but smile as Zoe turned away.

Despite the prim tone, he knew that she was tempted. And that, at least for now, was enough.

As she started toward the door, the sound of a sharp bark from outside, followed by a frenzy of barking, had her changing direction and heading over to the window.

"I don't believe it," she said. "There really are two of them."

He didn't need to peer over her shoulder to see what she was talking about—the barking had been a dead giveaway. But he crossed the room anyway, because it gave him an excuse to get closer to her and to watch the way her pulse skipped when she realized he was close.

"I warned you," he said.

Her lips curved. "Is his name really Guildenstern?"

"Yes, it is. And where there's Guildenstern, there's Tyler. C'mon," he said. "I'll introduce you."

He followed Zoe outside in time to see that his brother was just finishing up a phone call. Tyler tucked the cell into his pocket and crossed the yard in a few quick steps, an easy smile on his face.

"Tyler Sullivan," he said, ignoring his brother to offer his hand to Zoe.

She took his hand and gave him a smile. "Zoe Kozlowski."

"I was going to return your call today," he told her. "But since I had to come this way from another job, I thought I'd stop by." He continued to hold her hand as he lifted speculative blue eyes to meet the narrowed gaze of his brother hovering behind her. "I hope this isn't a bad time."

"Not at all," she said, finally extracting her fingers from his grasp. "I'm eager for you to take a look around, let me know if you're interested in the job."

"I'm definitely interested," Tyler said, and grinned in response to his brother's dark scowl.

"Keep looking at her like that and I'm going to have to pound on you," Mason warned, as he fell into step beside him.

The grin widened. "I'm thinking she would be worth it."

He cuffed his brother in the back of the head, just on principle.

It didn't take Mason long after Tyler had gone to finish tearing down the wall—at least what he could do with the rudimentary tools Zoe had on hand. But the open space seemed to open up endless possibilities, and he was pleased with the results when he carried his glass into the kitchen for a refill of the lemonade.

Zoe had been busy emptying out the cupboards, as attested by the pile of boxes stacked in the corner.

"I think you got the easier job," she grumbled as she rolled yet another piece of china in yet another sheet of newspaper.

"The less tedious one, anyway," he agreed.

He took the pitcher of lemonade out of the refrigerator.

"Did you want a drink?" he asked.

"Sure." She rolled her shoulders back then pointed to the cabinet over the sink. "There are still a couple of glasses in there. It occurred to me that I'd need to keep some dishes out if I actually wanted to eat."

"Good thinking." As he reached for a glass, a large manila envelope slid out of the cupboard and onto the counter.

Zoe sprang to her feet and grabbed the envelope, but not before he spotted the official emblem in the corner.

He poured her lemonade without saying a word.

She accepted the glass with murmured thanks.

"Well," he said after a long awkward moment had passed. "I think I understand now why you were trying to bash through that wall."

"Because it needed to be done," she said.

"You mean you weren't pretending to hammer your now ex-husband?"

She shook her head. "I told you before, it was an amicable split."

"Amicable doesn't mean painless."

"No." She set her glass on the counter and went back to wrapping and packing.

Obviously she didn't want to talk about it, and he considered just letting it go. But he saw defeat in the slump of her shoulders and sadness in her eyes.

Not his problem, he thought again. Except that it would take a stronger man than he was to walk away from a woman who was so obviously hurting. Instead of walking away, he laid his hands over hers, halting their quick, nervous movements.

"Are you okay?" he asked gently.

Zoe stared at Mason's hands—so strong and warm on hers—and nodded. It was the only response she could manage; the only one that was acceptable to her. She couldn't tell him that she was yearning for something new even while aching over the loss of what had been. She couldn't explain that her heart was pounding with anticipation while weeping with regrets.

"I am okay," she finally said. "I guess it's just harder to let go than it is to hold on sometimes, even when what you're holding on to isn't what you need anymore."

She pulled her hands away from his to reach for her glass and take a long drink.

"Our marriage started to fall apart a couple of years ago," she confided. "But I didn't want to admit it—I didn't want to fail. My mother's been married four times and in love more times than you can imagine. Each time, she swears he's the one—the final one, the only one. And he is—until the next one comes along.

"I didn't want to live my life like that. I promised myself I would only ever get married once and that it would be forever."

"It takes two people to make a marriage work," he pointed out. "Or fail."

She nodded. "I know. And I really believe we both wanted it to work—we just didn't know how. I guess I'm just sad that we failed, that the love we both felt so strongly in the beginning just faded away."

"So now you move on," he said, not unkindly. "You live the life you want to live and don't worry about pleasing anyone else."

"Sounds like a philosophy that would work really well on a desert island."

"Personal relationships do tend to complicate things," he admitted. "That's why I've never wanted to tie my life to someone else's, why I've been so careful to avoid any kind of entanglements. I refuse to depend on anyone else for my happiness."

"That sounds like the kind of absolute conviction that comes from having your heart broken."

"Or seeing what a broken heart can do to someone else," he said. "My parents were married for eighteen years, completely and indisputably in love with one another."

It was the bitterness in his tone that warned her the story didn't have a happy ending.

"Then my mother died," he said. "And my father was so overcome by grief, he eventually drank himself to death. He just couldn't bear to live without her."

"How old were you?"

"Sixteen when my mom died—almost twenty when my father was buried. Tyler's four years younger, so my grandmother—my mother's mom—moved in until he graduated high school. Then she married an RV salesman and moved down to Florida."

She smiled at that. "Is she still there?"

"Yeah. She's eighty-one now, her husband's eighty-four, and they recently celebrated their tenth anniversary."

There was both affection and amusement in his tone now, and it told her more than his words about the depth of his feelings for his grandmother.

"That's a nice story."

He brushed her bangs away from her face, his touch gentle. "You okay now?"

She nodded, and this time she meant it.

"Then I should be going."

The surprise must have shown on her face, because he smiled.

"Did you think I'd be all over you the minute your divorce was final?"

"No."

"Are you disappointed?"

"Of course not," she said, blushing.

He quirked an eyebrow. "Not even a little?"

"No," she lied.

He grinned. "You have been thinking about it, though."

"Thinking that it would be a bad idea," she told him.

"Which is why I'm willing to give you a little more time to accept the inevitability of it before I kiss you the way I've been thinking about doing."

Zoe didn't know how to respond to that without stuttering again, so she saved herself the embarrassment by remaining silent.

"Spending some time together away from the house might be a good start," he continued. "What do you think?"

"Are you asking me to go on a date?"

"*Date* is too formal a word for what I had in mind."

"What did you have in mind?"

"Fishing."

She shook her head. "No."

"Why not?"

"Because."

"That's not a reason," he chided. "Do you have other plans for tomorrow?"

"No, but—"

"I'll pick you up at six, we can grab breakfast on the way."

"Six o'clock? In the morning?" She stared at him. "Are you insane?"

"It's a bit of a drive to the lake, so we might as well get an early start."

"I don't want to get an early start or a late start or any kind of start," she said. "Because I don't want to go fishing."

He touched a hand to her cheek. "I'd like to spend the day with you."

And that easily, he obliterated all of her protests.

Chapter Seven

"I don't get this fishing thing," Zoe said as she followed Mason through the long grass toward what he'd promised was a prime location on the lake.

"What's not to get?"

"Well, you admitted that the number of fish in the lake has been dwindling over the past few years and that you don't usually keep the ones you catch, anyway. So what's the point?"

"The point is to relax," he said with exaggerated patience as he continued down the overgrown path.

"Relax? I have flower beds to weed, a porch to sand, a gazebo to paint—and those are only the jobs at the top of the list."

"Which is all the more reason that you need to do

something like this," he pointed out. "You've been working almost nonstop since you moved in."

"I still can't believe I let you talk me into this," she muttered.

"You couldn't resist the opportunity to be with me," he teased.

She shook her head as the beast, who had raced ahead as soon as Mason opened the door of the SUV, let out a sharp bark.

"And Rosie, of course," he added, and grinned.

"I know why you invited me, though," she said. "So that I could carry all the gear."

"I've got our lunch."

And she knew the cooler he was lugging was a lot heavier than the rods and tackle box in her hands. But the long poles were awkward to handle and kept whacking against low-hanging branches or, when she shifted her hold so they weren't sticking up into the air, getting tangled in the long weeds.

At last they came to the clearing, and Zoe had to admit it was a pretty spot. There was a grassy bank dotted with wildflowers that sloped down toward the rocky shore of a clear blue lake.

"The lake's quite deep here, so we can drop our lines right from the shore."

"Did I mention that I don't know how to fish?"

"The look on your face when I mentioned fishing was a pretty good hint." He set the cooler under the shade of a tree, then came over to take the poles and tackle box from her. "That's why I brought you a closed-face reel—it's easy to cast and unlikely to tangle.

You just hold down the button as you draw your arm back, then release it when you cast toward the water."

"Piece of cake," she said.

He smiled. "You'll get the hang of it quickly—I promise."

She had to give him credit for patience. He took his time explaining every step of the process, though a lot of what he said was lost on Zoe when he held her close, her back against his front, to demonstrate the proper casting procedure.

But after several unsuccessful attempts, she finally managed to land the baited hook in the water rather than on the grassy bank.

"Good," he said, then set about preparing his own gear.

"Why don't you have one of those little ball things on yours?" she asked after he'd cast his line.

"Because I don't need one."

She frowned at that. "Why do I need one?"

"Because you've never done this before so you might not realize what's happening when a fish is tugging on your line. The bobber being pulled into the water will let you know."

"And what do I do when the bobber goes in the water?"

"You tug on the pole to make sure the fish is hooked, then you reel it in."

"Okay. The bobber goes down, I pull up, then reel in."

"That's right." He finished reeling his own line back in, then tossed it out again.

"How long does it usually take to catch a fish?"

"There's no 'usual,'" he said. "Sometimes you catch one, sometimes you don't."

"You mean I might not catch a fish today?"

"You definitely won't if you don't stop talking and starting fishing."

"My line's in the water," she pointed out.

"Then sit down and get comfortable."

"You're not sitting. And you keep reeling in and casting out again. How come?"

"Because some fish are more likely to take bait that's moving."

"Then why did you tell me to leave mine in the water?"

"Because I thought it would be easier for you to relax that way."

She sat down, braced her forearms on her bent knees, the end of the pole cradled between her hands. "Where's Rosie gone?"

"Exploring."

"You don't worry that he'll take off?"

"He never has before."

She stared at the red-and-white ball floating on the water. "I think it moved."

"What moved?"

"The bobber thing."

He shook his head. "Could you maybe signal before you change direction in a conversation?"

"Do I pull up now?" she wanted to know.

He shook his head. "It's just drifting along with the movement of the water. It needs to be pulled under the surface."

"Oh." She continued to watch the floating ball. "How is this supposed to be relaxing?"

She thought his sigh sounded a little less patient

now. "You know, I think I liked you better an hour ago when you were still half-asleep and not talking."

"I had coffee at the diner."

"And?"

"Caffeine revs me."

"Now I understand the pink tea," he muttered.

"Anyway, I thought you invited me to come fishing with you so we could talk."

"I distinctly remember saying 'fishing' not 'talking.'"

"Why do the two have to be mutually exclusive?"

"Do you even know how to sit back and clear your mind?"

"Clear my mind?"

"Yeah. Do you think you can handle that?"

She frowned. "No. Because now I'm thinking that I'm supposed to be relaxing and…"

The words trailed off as he dropped to the ground beside her. He put his pole aside, then took the one from her hands and set it down, too.

"What are you doing?"

"Helping to clear your mind."

And then his mouth was on hers.

She didn't have time to think or prepare or defend. She didn't have time to do anything but absorb the lovely shock that sparked at the first touch, then yield to the mastery of the kiss as those skilled and hungry lips moved over hers.

Later, she would think about how fast he'd moved—and how he'd taken his time. How his mouth cruised over hers, his exploration patient, unhurried—and very,

very thorough. How he traced the shape of her mouth with the tip of his tongue and nibbled gently on the full curve of her bottom lip. How she could do nothing but sigh—and surrender to the pleasure.

Her blood heated. Her head spun.

Her body yearned.

He cradled her face in his hands, his touch gentle but unyielding as he held her captive to the onslaught of his mouth. She lifted her hands, curled them around his wrists and felt the rapid beat of his pulse, echoing her own heartbeat. Everything else faded away into dreamy layers of mist and fog.

She didn't know how long he kissed her, just that it seemed like forever but not nearly long enough. And when his lips finally eased way, she nearly whimpered in protest.

"What are you thinking about now, Zoe?" The question was a whisper against her lips.

"Huh?" She blinked, tried to focus, but everything was as soft and nebulous as a dream. "What?"

His lips curved slowly, smugly.

"Good answer," he said, and kissed her again until her mind was spinning like a fishing reel when the line was being cast.

Then he turned away from her, picked up his pole again and tossed his line into the lake as if the kiss had never happened.

Mason wished the kiss had never happened.

As he shifted his rod from one hand to the other, he cursed himself for including a woman in what had always before been a solitary venture. She'd been on his mind a lot lately—which was one of the reasons he'd planned to come fishing today, to get away, empty his head and relax. Now he was more tightly wound than his line—and aching to release some of the tension.

He glanced sideways at Zoe. She was sitting cross-legged on the grass now, the reel of her fishing pole cupped loosely between her palms, her gaze focused intently on the water. She was also, he noted, quiet.

He wondered if he should apologize for kissing her, then decided it was ridiculous to apologize for something he already wanted to do again. He had yet to decide whether or not he would give in to that urge.

He might wish it had never happened, but he wasn't sorry he'd kissed her. He was only sorry that he'd pushed after promising to give her time. He hadn't intended to move so fast. He knew she needed to mourn and accept the loss of her marriage before she'd be ready to move on. Wasn't that why he'd invited her to come with him today? Because he knew she was hurting and needed a distraction.

Instead, she'd turned out to *be* a hell of a distraction.

Because though he might have moved faster than he'd intended, she sure didn't seem to have any problem keeping pace. From the moment his lips had touched hers, it had been like setting a match to dry tinder—immediate flame and intense heat.

He was surprised by how out-of-control he felt. Even as a teenager, he'd never wanted anyone as much as he wanted Zoe right now. Then again, there had been a lot of other stuff going on in his life when he was a teenager, and he hadn't had much time for dating. He'd spent too many months watching his mother die, pleading and praying that she wouldn't, then too many years after she was gone trying to hold his father back from the brink of self-destruction. He'd failed on all accounts.

He didn't blame himself. He knew he wasn't responsible for either the disease that had eaten away at his mother or the sorrow that had consumed his father, but he was undeniably affected by the loss of both of his parents in such a short period of time. Though Gord Sullivan had held on for four more years after his wife's death, for all intents and purposes, he was gone from his family as soon as he buried his beloved Elaine. Mason saw how his father's grief had slowly but inexorably destroyed not just the quality of his life but his will to live, and he had vowed that he would never let himself feel that kind of devastation. He would never be that vulnerable. He would never love so wholly and completely.

But somehow Zoe made him forget all of his resolutions. She made him forget logic and reason. Hell, he couldn't even seem to think when she was around—except about how much he wanted her.

Part of it was sexual attraction—pure and simple. But the rest of it wasn't so simple. He didn't just want her, he wanted to be *with* her. He wanted to spend time with her, talking to her, laughing with her or even just sitting quietly with her.

She was just a woman, like so many other women he'd known. And yet, she was somehow different.

Because no other woman had got under his skin the way she'd done. No other woman had plagued his mind during the day or haunted his dreams at night. He'd always managed to maintain an emotional distance, but it seemed to be a losing battle with Zoe. Maybe for the first time in his life, he was truly falling for a woman, and he didn't know how to handle it—or even if he wanted to.

At their initial meeting, Zoe's first impression of Tyler Sullivan had been that he bore a striking resemblance to his brother—not just in the color of his hair and his eyes or the wide shoulders and long, lean build, but in the way his mouth curved just a little bit higher on one side than the other when he smiled, and in the way his eyes sparked with interest or humor. He was undeniably good-looking, irresistibly charming and outrageously flirtatious.

Her second thought was that he seemed young to be running a successful building company. But a few discreet inquiries had confirmed the reputation of Pinehurst Rehab and so she'd hired him.

In the two weeks since he'd started the renovations on Hadfield House, she'd had no cause to regret that decision. In fact, with each day that passed and each job that was completed, she'd only been more impressed with his work ethic. He came early, stayed late, and could frequently be found working right alongside his crew. He didn't seem to mind when she peeked in to see how things were coming along, and he answered her questions patiently and thoroughly.

If he occasionally lingered to flirt with her after the other men were gone—as he sometimes did—she couldn't help but feel flattered even if she knew better than to take him too seriously.

"What's the scoop with you and my brother?" Tyler asked, leaning against the kitchen counter with a can of soda in his hand.

Zoe passed him a plate with two sandwiches and a pile of potato chips. It was a Sunday and while the rest of his crew had been given the day off, Tyler had come by to install a couple of replacement windows. She figured the least she could do was to make him lunch.

"I'm not sure I understand the question."

"Do you have a relationship with my brother?"

"He's my neighbor, obviously," she said. "But I like to think that he's also become a friend."

"Friend?" Tyler laughed.

She frowned and munched on a chip. "Why is that funny?"

"Because when I told him I was coming over to put in your windows, my brother made it very clear I wasn't to touch anything else."

Zoe felt her cheeks flush. "I'm sure you misunderstood."

"Then you're not sleeping with him?"

"Tyler!"

He grinned. "You don't have to answer that question."

He was completely outrageous and somehow disarmingly charming. "You're way off base on this. Your brother's interested in the house—not me."

"The house has great bones," he said. "But you have much nicer curves."

She laughed. "And you have even more in common with your brother than I originally thought."

"If you mean we have great taste in women, I'd have to agree."

"I mean that you're arrogant, charming and outrageous."

Tyler grinned. "We do have a lot in common—which is how I know he's interested. Because you can bet that if I'd seen you first, I'd be making a move."

"Well, I don't know what seeing me first has to do with it, but I can assure you that he hasn't made a move." She thought of the kiss at the lake, the kiss that had made everything inside her melt into a gooey puddle of need, and dismissed it. Because that kiss—as knock-your-socks-off fabulous as it had been for Zoe—had obviously meant nothing to Mason because he hadn't even attempted a repeat performance.

Tyler narrowed his gaze on her, as if he knew she was holding something back. "He hasn't?"

"He kissed me once," she admitted. "But that was a few weeks ago now, so I have to assume that if he was interested, he isn't anymore."

"Then maybe he's not as smart as I thought." He carried his empty plate to the sink, then turned, sandwiching her between the counter at her back and his body at her front. "And maybe I was wrong to worry that I would be poaching."

"Poaching?" she queried.

He lifted a shoulder.

"He means trespassing." Mason's voice—tinged with annoyance—interrupted from the doorway. "And yes, you are."

Tyler winked at her before turning around. In that moment, Zoe knew that he'd known Mason was in the doorway when he'd asked about her relationship with his brother.

"It looks like you finished the windows," Mason told him.

"Sure did."

"Then beat it."

"I'll see you tomorrow, Zoe," Tyler said, unfazed by his brother's rudeness. "Thanks for lunch."

"Thanks for giving up your day off to put the windows in."

"Not a problem," he said, and sauntered unhurriedly out the door.

Zoe waited until she heard Tyler's truck start up before she spoke to Mason. "You were rude."

"He was poaching," he said simply.

"Poaching?" she echoed again, then shook her head. "I know what it means, I'm just having a little trouble understanding it in this context."

"It means that you were wrong in assuming I was no longer interested." He slid his hands around her waist and drew her into the circle of his arms.

"I haven't seen much of you over the past couple of weeks."

"Miss me?"

"No," she lied weakly.

"I missed you," he said, and settled his mouth over hers.

She was prepared for his kiss this time, but still unprepared for the slow burning need that spread through her body in response to the kiss.

She'd dated casually and infrequently in college, then she'd married Scott right after graduation. In the past nine years, she'd only been kissed by her husband. When the marriage had fallen apart, or maybe for the reasons it had fallen apart, she'd never expected to want like this again. But as his lips continued to move over hers, she couldn't deny that she wanted Mason.

She wanted to touch and be touched, to give and to take, to once again feel the pleasure of passion. What made her want even more was that she'd dreamed about it—about making love with Mason. Frequently and in glorious, mind-numbing detail. And she'd been haunted by those dreams as much awake as asleep.

But in her dreams, everything was soft and misty and perfect. In her dreams, her body was warm and soft and responsive. In her dreams, she was happy, almost giddy, free of any inhibitions and all physical and emotional scars.

Unfortunately, her reality was different.

He said he wanted her. He kissed her as if he would never stop, touched her as if he'd never get enough. But he didn't know what she'd been through; he couldn't understand what he was getting into if they were to become physically involved.

She'd left Manhattan because her life had been irrevocably altered and, in making that decision, she'd acknowledged that some of her goals would have to change, some of her dreams had been lost. She certainly hadn't ever expected to want to open up her heart to a man again.

Then Mason Sullivan had stormed into her life and through the barriers she'd so carefully erected. He tempted her with warm eyes and hot kisses. He made her want things she had no business wanting, made her long for things she knew she could never have.

But now, as she felt the evidence of his arousal against her and the answering aching heat of her own desire, she wondered. He made her weak with wanting and empowered her with the knowledge that he wanted her, too. To be desired now, by this man, was a heady experience and she wanted to glory in it. Except that he didn't really want her—he wanted the woman he thought she was, and she hadn't been that woman for a long time.

Though her body protested at even the thought of ending this intimacy, she forced herself to pull away.

"That's why I've been trying to stay away," Mason told her, catching his breath. "Because when I'm with you, I can't help wanting you. And when I touch you, I don't want to stop."

"I'm really not ready for this."

He stroked a hand over her hair. "We'll take it slow."

She shook her head again. "I can't—I don't—" she let out an exasperated breath as her brain scrambled for an explanation he would accept—anything but the truth. At last she said, "I want us to be friends."

"We are friends."

"*Just* friends."

He smiled, then he touched his mouth to hers again in a kiss that was both unhurried and unrelenting, and she was helpless to do anything but respond.

This time *he* stepped back. "We'll take it slow," he said again.

Before she could say anything else, he was gone.

Outside of Pinehurst, miles beyond the wide rolling fields of farmland that bordered the easternmost edge of the town, there was an enormous old barn that was referred to by locals simply as "the old barn." It was sometimes used as an auction house, occasionally as a community gathering space, but had gained notoriety for the flea market that was held there every Sunday. And every Sunday, seemingly regardless of the time of year or the weather, it was packed to bursting with vendors hawking their wares and customers looking for bargains.

Zoe and Claire eased their way through the crowd, from stalls set up with orderly rows of homemade jellies and jams to makeshift tables heaped with knock-off Rolex watches, through towering shelves filled with old and new books past booths of glossy handcrafted furniture, between glass showcases of exquisite antique jewelry and freestanding displays offering the latest in household gadgets.

The air was rich with the scents of damp earth, musty hay and fresh caramel corn.

Zoe was munching on a handful of the sweet, salty treat as she followed her friend through the maze of chaos to a table displaying handmade linens. She'd been looking forward to this outing since Claire had called to suggest it a few days before, not just because she loved the atmosphere of the market but also because she wanted to talk to her friend about something that had been tugging at her mind. She hadn't counted on the noise and the crowd making conversation so difficult, and she took advantage of the relative quiet of the corner to finally say, "I'm thinking of having an affair."

Claire traced the edging of a Battenburg lace tablecloth and nodded approvingly. "Good for you."

Zoe frowned.

Her friend sent her a sidelong glance. "Did you think I'd be shocked?"

"*I'm* shocked," she admitted. "I've never considered anything like this before."

"You've been married for the past nine years," Claire reminded her.

Zoe nodded. Scott was the first man she'd ever been with. She'd never imagined being with anyone else, had certainly never had sexual fantasies about any other man.

Until Mason.

She could ignore it, deny it, pretend the attraction she felt didn't exist, but she couldn't will it away. The heart-pounding, mind-numbing passion she felt when he kissed her was new and unfamiliar. If she'd ever felt the same dizzying rush of excitement and anticipation with Scott—and she wanted to believe that she had—it had been a long time ago, so far back in her memory that what she felt with Mason now seemed enticingly new, completely unfamiliar and dangerously tempting.

"I think part of what makes this so strange," she

said, "is that I've never been really attracted to anyone but Scott."

"That is strange," Claire agreed. "Were you in a marriage or a convent? Because I love my husband, but a wink or a smile from a good-looking man can still make my heart go pitter-patter."

"My heart doesn't go pitter-patter," she admitted. "It pounds so hard inside my chest I wonder that my ribs don't crack."

Her friend smiled. "Yeah, I can see how Mason Sullivan could have that effect on a woman."

"I never said it was Mason."

"The only other man whose name I've heard you mention is Harry Anderson, and he's a little old for you, not to mention married with four kids and a grand-child on the way."

"Okay—it is Mason." She hesitated a moment before asking, "Did he have that effect on you?"

Her friend checked the price tag, sighed with obvious regret and carefully refolded the item.

"Hmm?" Claire moved on to a set of doilies.

"When you were dating Mason? Did your heart pound like that?"

"No. For me it was nothing more than the pitter-patter." She frowned as they moved away from the doilies. "Come to think of it, the only man who ever made me feel that kind of pulse-racing excitement was Rob."

"Why are you saying that as if it's a bad thing?"

"It's not—for me. But it makes me worry that you might be falling in love with Mason instead of just falling into bed with him."

She shook her head. "I won't—one heartbreak in this lifetime is enough."

Claire turned to study her closely, then sighed. "Honey, that dreamy look in your eyes tells me that you're already halfway there."

Zoe sifted through a bin of ceramic knobs, searching for something that would work with the new bathroom cabinets she'd picked out. "We came here last weekend," she said. "To look for lamps for what is going to be the library."

"He went shopping with you? Without any bribes or threats involved?"

"It was actually his idea."

"Oh. Well." Claire smiled now. "Maybe you're not the only one who's halfway there."

"We were shopping for lighting, not diamonds," she pointed out dryly.

"Rob hates coming here," her friend mused, almost to herself. "The parking is terrible, the crowds drive him insane. He'll come—if I ask. But he'd certainly never suggest it himself."

She shrugged. "I think Mason just knew what I was looking for and thought we might be able to find it here."

"Did you?"

"I got a couple of brass lamps with beaded shades. They're fabulous." She found a gorgeous cut-glass doorknob she couldn't resist even though she didn't know where she would use it. "Oh, and Mason picked up a turn-of-the-century mantle clock."

"I think maybe you found something else, too," Claire said.

"What's that?" Zoe asked, taking some bills from her wallet to pay for her purchase.

Her friend grinned. "A man who just might be worth the risk of falling in love again."

Chapter Eight

Zoe turned down Mason's invitation to celebrate the Fourth of July with friends at his home. Not because she didn't want to spend the day with him, but because she was afraid of how much she *did* want to. They'd been spending a lot of time together lately, shared more than a few sizzling kisses, and though there was a part of her that very much wanted to take that next step, there was another part that just wasn't ready.

He'd been surprised by her refusal, maybe even disappointed, but he hadn't tried to persuade her otherwise. Not really. He'd just shrugged and told her to stop by if she changed her mind.

She changed her mind more than a dozen times over the next couple of days, but in the end resolved to take a step back until she knew for sure what she wanted—and that she could give him what she knew he wanted. So when Claire called and invited her to spend the day with her family, Zoe jumped at the opportunity. Anything to get her away from the house and the temptation of Mason's invitation.

She didn't realize, until Rob pulled his van into the driveway just down the street from her own, that her best friend had conspired to thwart her plans.

It would be simple enough to climb out of the vehicle, walk right back down the driveway and go home. But as quickly as the thought crossed her mind, it was discarded. Doing so would be both childish and unappreciative of the effort Mason had made to get her here.

Instead, she picked up the bowl of potato salad she'd made and carried it toward the house.

Mason opened the door in response to her knock. His quick smile of greeting faded when he heard the pounding of paws behind him.

Zoe gripped the bowl in her hands tighter, bracing herself for the attack.

"Rosie, down."

At Mason's sharp command, the dog immediately dropped to the ground, his belly on the floor, his tongue hanging out of his mouth as he whined plaintively.

"Now that's a well-trained dog," Rob commented.

Zoe snorted, though she bent to pat Rosie's head, acknowledging his obedience.

"We're working on it," Mason said, and held out his hand. "You must be Claire's husband."

As introductions were made, she moved into the kitchen to put the salad in the refrigerator.

She heard Mason ask Claire and Rob and the kids what they wanted to drink, then sent them out to the backyard. "Down the hall, through the patio doors. Basically, just follow the noise," he told them.

Zoe turned as she closed the refrigerator door and bumped into Mason's chest. He caught her around the waist before she could back away.

"I thought you had other plans for today," he said.

"So did I, not realizing when I accepted Claire's invitation to join her family for a barbecue at a friend's house that you were the friend."

"Would it have made a difference?"

"Yes," she admitted. "Because most of the people here are *your* friends, and I didn't want to give them the wrong impression about us."

"What is the wrong impression, Zoe?"

"That we're…together."

He slid his arms up her back. "And why is that wrong?"

"Because we're not," she insisted, aware of how ridiculous her argument sounded when she was still in the circle of his arms. "And you need to let me go before someone walks in."

"I will," he said, but drew her nearer. "As soon as I say a proper hello."

"Hello," he whispered the word against her lips.

"Hi."

Then he was kissing her softly, slowly and very thoroughly.

"I'm glad you decided to come, Zoe."

"I didn't seem to have much choice."

He cupped her face between his palms. "You always have a choice, Zoe."

She knew he was referring to more than her decision to stay for the barbecue. She also knew that it wasn't true.

Because her feelings for him were already stronger than she would have chosen. She'd been thinking about having an affair, not falling in love. But Claire was right—she was already halfway there and dangerously close to tumbling the rest of the way.

It was a good turnout, Mason thought, as he surveyed the collection of people around the backyard.

Nick and Jessica were there, with baby Libby, who was now six weeks old and, impossible as it seemed, even cuter than the last time he'd seen her. Nick's sister, Kristin, her husband, Brian, and Caleb, the youngest of their three children, had also come out. Then there was the Lamontagne family: Claire and Rob and their children, Jason and Laurel. It turned out that Jason played on the same baseball team as Caleb, so the boys were already acquainted, and Laurel, though nearly three years younger than the two boys, didn't have any trouble keeping up.

Tyler had been the last to arrive, and he'd come without a date this year, which was unusual. He had, however, brought Stern to play with Rosie, and the two dogs were tearing through the yard like they were being chased by the hounds of hell instead of three screaming children.

But it was Zoe to whom Mason's attention was drawn throughout the day.

He was pleased to have her here, with all of his friends. But he was already looking forward to later, when those friends would be gone and he could be alone with her.

Right now she was playing volleyball in the pool with the kids—and Tyler, of course. Ty had been hovering around Zoe for most of the day, but in a protective brotherly way that didn't worry Mason in the least. Though Tyler was a lot closer to Zoe's age than he was, Mason could tell by the easy way they interacted that their relationship was strictly platonic. Zoe wasn't nearly as comfortable around him, and he realized he didn't want her to be. He wanted her aware and interested, and he knew she was both, even if she continued to fight the attraction that flared whenever they were together.

A round of high-fives among the members of the winning team—not Zoe's—indicated that the game was over. Mason watched her swim to the stairs at the edge of the pool and climb out. He watched as she rubbed a towel over her body, over her arms, her legs, her bare midriff. The red halter-style bikini top cradled her breasts and displayed just a shadowy hint of cleavage. The low-rise bottoms dipped a couple of inches below her belly button and highlighted the sweet curve of her buttocks.

He was pleased when she came over to the patio where he'd dropped into a lounge chair to take a break from the various activities going on. She took a can of 7UP from the cooler, popped the top.

"Who won at horseshoes?" she asked.

"Me and Rob."

She sat down across from him and smiled. "Did I thank you for inviting them today?"

"No," he said. "But there's no need to. I thought you'd be more comfortable with some of your own friends here."

"And you're not uncomfortable with one of your ex-girlfriends here?"

"Are you uncomfortable with the fact that I dated Claire?"

"No." But she didn't meet his gaze. "Not really. I mean, I know it was a long time ago, before I knew either of you. It's just…weird."

"I never slept with her, Zoe."

"I didn't ask."

He smiled. "But you were wondering."

"Maybe," she allowed after a moment's pause.

"In fact, if I remember correctly, we didn't go beyond the holding-hands-kiss-good-night stage."

"Oh."

"Does that make it a little less weird?"

She shrugged. "It's really none of my business."

"Sure it is," he told her. "Because I *am* going to sleep with you."

"That's still undecided."

He leaned forward to tip her chin up with his finger and had the pleasure of watching her eyes go dark, wary.

"Only the 'when' is undecided," he promised her, and brushed his lips over hers, light and easy.

Her eyes remained open, wary, though the hitch in her breath gave her away.

Keeping it easy, he tapped a finger to the end of her nose. "You should have a hat on. Your skin's turning pink."

"I, uh—" she blinked, drew away. "I have sunscreen on. I didn't bring a hat."

"There's a baseball cap on the top shelf of the hall closet," he told her. "Go get it so your pretty skin doesn't burn."

Zoe went to get the hat. Partly because it wasn't something that she figured was worth standing on the patio and arguing with him about. And partly because it seemed like a good excuse to make a strategic retreat from any discussion about their relationship.

He was so confident about the direction in which they were headed, and she was still so uncertain—and feeling guilty about being uncertain. But she didn't know what she wanted. Or maybe she did know, but knew that what she wanted most—a family like Claire and Rob's or Kristin and Brian's or Jessica and Nick's—she couldn't have.

She shook off the thought and ignored the yearning as she moved through the house. She paused when she saw Jessica curled up at one end of the sofa in the living room with her baby. In the soft glow of the afternoon sun, she looked like a Madonna with child—beautiful, peaceful, ethereal.

Zoe didn't mean to stare, but she couldn't seem to look away. And as the baby suckled hungrily at her mother's breast, she felt a phantom tug in her own breasts, and a sharp pang of longing deep in her heart.

But she felt something else, too. Something she hadn't felt in a very long time—the desire for a camera in her hand, the need to capture a beautiful, timeless moment that would never exist precisely like this again.

Then she glanced down and it was there, and her fingers reached instinctively toward it.

She'd had legitimate reasons for walking away from her career, although the decision hadn't been made without a certain amount of remorse and regret. She'd been saddened by everything she'd lost and, in her determination to start her life over, she'd cut out the good parts with the bad.

Maybe, she thought now, it was time to re-evaluate.

She set the camera down again and ducked back out of the doorway, making her way to the closet to get the hat Mason had sent her inside to find...and to dry the tears that were on her cheeks.

When Zoe walked past the barbecue where he'd started to cook dinner, Mason couldn't resist yanking on the ponytail that was pulled through the keyhole at the back of his Carolina Hurricanes baseball cap.

"Hey," she protested when he tugged on her hair.

"You look so cute, I couldn't resist."

She wrinkled her nose. "Cute?"

"The hat's a good look for you," Rob said, stepping into the conversation. "Except for your choice of teams."

"It's my hat," Mason told them.

"I'm a Rangers fan from way back, but I have to admit it was an exciting finish when the Canes took the Stanley Cup in oh-six," Brian said.

"The Stanley Cup?" Zoe's brows drew together. "Isn't that hockey?"

Mason didn't miss the looks of shock and horror that passed between the other men in response to Zoe's question.

"She doesn't watch sports," he explained. Then, to Zoe, "Yes, it's the ultimate prize in hockey."

"So how could a baseball team win the Stanley Cup?"

Tyler shook his head, choking back his laughter. "The Carolina Hurricanes are a hockey team, honey."

"Then why is their logo on a baseball cap?" she challenged.

And, without waiting for an answer, she turned and walked away.

Mason couldn't help but grin at her bizarre logic as he watched her make her way over to the pool.

"Well." Rob seemed at a loss for words.

"Not his usual type, that's for sure," Brian said.

"So what do you and Zoe talk about when you're together?" Nick wondered. "Because you're obviously not discussing the pennant race."

"All kinds of things," Mason said. "Books and movies, world news and current events."

"Whether the Belter rosewood sofa would work better in the front parlor or the library," Tyler interjected.

"The parlor," Mason said. "With the balloon-back side chairs."

"See?" Tyler said. "They spend all their time together moving furniture around, hanging wallpaper, shopping for window coverings."

"So I'm helping her out with some things," Mason said, aware that he sounded just a little bit defensive. "What's the big deal?"

"The big deal is that I was actually starting to think it would never happen," Nick said.

"Thought what would never happen?"

"You falling in love," Tyler said.

Mason choked on a mouthful of beer.

Brian thumped him on the back, a little harder than was really necessary.

"This his first time?" Rob asked, in obvious disbelief.

Mason watched his friends all nod; he scowled.

"It's not happening this time," he said firmly.

"I have to agree with your friends on this," Rob said. "All outward indications are that you're hooked."

He shook his head.

"You just don't have the experience to recognize it," Brian added. "But we do."

His friends all nodded their agreement.

"But don't worry." Nick clapped a hand on his shoulder. "Zoe doesn't seem to be looking for all of that happily-ever-after stuff most women want. I'm sure it's only a matter of time before she cuts you loose."

He wanted to insist that he wasn't hooked, and at the same time, he wanted to demand to know why—if he was hooked—Zoe would cut him loose.

"Besides," Rob added, "I can't imagine she wants to stay around here in the long term."

Somehow the suggestion was more alarming than reassuring. "Has she said something about leaving?" Mason wanted to know.

"No, but it makes sense that she'd head back to Manhattan after the renovations are complete."

Mason scowled and tipped his bottle to his lips.

Zoe hadn't said anything to him about leaving Pine-hurst. Then again, she hadn't said anything at all about her long-term plans. Of course, he hadn't asked because it wasn't any of his business. He didn't do long-term.

Still, he was pretty confident that if he put his mind to it, he could convince her to stay.

It wasn't too long after dinner that the crowd started to thin out.

Nick and Jessica begged off before the fireworks started, worried that the noise might be too much for Libby. Kristin, Brian and Caleb were the next to leave, after the display of lights and rockets was concluded. Then Claire and Rob and their kids headed out imme-diately afterward. And when Tyler disappeared on the pretext of having somewhere else to go, Zoe and Mason were alone.

"I seem to have, uh, lost my ride," she said.

He smiled. "I'll make sure you get home later."

"It's late already."

"Not so late." He poked a stick into the fire, adjust-ing the logs. "You have somewhere you need to be early in the morning?"

"No," she admitted.

"Then stay," he said. "For a while."

He couldn't know how tempted she was, how much she wanted to be with him in every way. But as fierce as the needs were inside of her, the nerves were just as strong.

If they became lovers, he would be the first since her husband had left. The first to see her naked. The first to see her scars. As much as her body yearned for the fulfillment of physical intimacy, her heart wasn't ready to risk it.

"We could go skinny-dipping under the stars," he said.

"Or we could keep our clothes on and roast marshmallows by the fire."

He shrugged. "It doesn't sound like as much fun as skinny-dipping, but okay."

"Do you have any more marshmallows?" she asked, noting that the package he'd opened for the kids was completely empty.

"Yeah." He rose to his feet. "Kristin brought a couple of bags."

While he went inside, she waited by the fire, staring at the flames and worrying that her agreement to stay— even for a little while—would result in her getting burned.

She was a rational woman—careful, organized, logical. She liked schedules and routines, certainty and predictability. At least, that's what she used to believe. Then she'd had an impulse—buy a house. Not just any house, but a beat-up Victorian mansion that she felt needed her as much as she needed a purpose.

It was one spontaneous act that seemed to have turned her whole world upside down. Not twenty-four hours after moving into that house, she'd met Mason Sullivan—and her world had been spinning out of control ever since.

She was scared—out of her league and over her head and so many other clichés. She wanted her life back on track and the ground solid beneath her feet. Mostly, she admitted on a sigh, she wanted Mason.

When she glanced up and saw him striding across the lawn, her heart did that funny little roll in her chest that was becoming all too familiar, and she sighed again.

As he drew nearer, she noticed that he carried not just the marshmallows but a couple bottles of beer. She shook her head when he offered one to her.

"Thanks, but my head is already fuzzy." Although she wasn't sure if it was the beer or Mason's presence that was responsible for that effect, she was erring on the side of caution.

He sank down to the ground beside her and grinned. "Are you worried that I'll get you drunk and try to seduce you?"

"No," she said. "Because we both know that if you really wanted me in your bed, I'd already be there."

"I really want you in my bed," he said, and the huskiness in his tone assured her it was true. "I'm just waiting until you're sure that you want to be there."

"It's not that simple," she said, sliding a marshmallow onto the end of her stick and carefully positioning it close to the glowing embers of the fire.

"It could be," he said, placing his stick directly into the fire.

She shook her head as the edges of the marshmallow quickly heated, bubbled, then burst into flames.

He pulled the stick back, blew out the fire, then plucked the charred remains from the point and popped it into his mouth.

She continued to turn her stick, evenly toasting her marshmallow all the way around.

Mason stuck a second marshmallow into the fire.

"You obviously don't believe that patience is a virtue," she noted.

He shrugged. "I just want what I want when I want it."

"And I like to take my time," she said, finally judging her marshmallow to be done. "To make sure that it's really what I want and not some passing fancy."

"But if you wait too long—" he said, stealing the lightly toasted marshmallow off the end of her stick "—you might find that someone else has already taken what you wanted."

"Hey."

He held it away from her. "You want this?"

She responded by snatching it back.

Mason grinned as she bit into the marshmallow.

The outside was crisp, the inside gooey—just the way she liked them. She closed her eyes and hummed with approval as the sugary taste exploded on her tongue.

"Good?" he asked.

She nodded and offered him the rest.

He took her hand and brought it to his mouth to nip the last bite, then licked the remaining traces of marshmallow from her fingers. His tongue swiped the pad of her finger, then her thumb, then he sucked it into his mouth.

Arrows of heat rocketed through her system, straight to her core, and everything inside her melted like the marshmallow she'd just eaten.

His lips closed over her thumb, then slid away.

"I think I need another taste," he said.

Then his mouth was on hers, hot and hungry. And her mouth was just as hot, just as hungry. When his tongue speared deep inside, she welcomed the thrust, absorbed the passion. He tasted hot and sweet from the marshmallows, and incredibly and temptingly male.

The fire was starting to burn down, but the heat between them continued to rise as he eased her back onto the grass. He was stretched out beside her, his hands skimming over her, from the curve of her shoulders to the slope of her breasts, to the dip in her waist to the flare of her hips.

She was burning everywhere he touched, aching. She wanted to press her body against his and wrap her legs around him. She wanted to touch and taste and take. She simply wanted.

If she'd been able to think, she might have been shocked by the fierceness of the desire, the rawness of the need. But she couldn't think, she could only feel, and it felt wonderful to have his hands on hers, to have hers on him.

With every pass of those wide palms, her pulse rocketed, her senses scrambled, her body yearned.

She was overwhelmed by the sensations he evoked. Heat and hunger. Desires and demands. Nerves and needs.

His hand was beneath the hem of her T-shirt now, his fingertips skimming over the bare skin of her tummy, teasing, testing. Then tracing over the ridges of her rib cage to the swell of her breast.

Her nipple puckered as his thumb brushed over the wisp of lace that covered it, and spears of fiery heat shot to her core. She gasped and arched toward him, wanting more, wanting everything. His searching fingers moved to the centre clasp of her bra, dipped into the hollow between her breasts.

Later, she would be grateful for the rocket that was set off somewhere down the street, for the sharp crack of the explosion that finally penetrated the haze of lust that clouded her brain.

She pushed herself up, her breath coming in unsteady gasps as she fought to clear her mind and silence the indignant protests of her body.

To her complete and utter bafflement, Mason didn't move closer or protest her withdrawal in any way. Instead, he stroked a hand over her hair.

"I'm sorry."

She almost laughed, but she was afraid it might somehow set free the tears she was trying so desperately to hold in check. "Why are you sorry?"

"Because I promised we could take it slow, and I keep forgetting that in my eagerness to get you naked."

His patience and understanding only made her feel worse, because she couldn't guarantee that she would ever be ready to take that next step—and she couldn't tell him what was holding her back.

She stood up, tugged her T-shirt into place and slipped her feet back into her sandals. "I have to go."

Of course, he insisted on walking her home, and she didn't bother to protest.

When they reached her door and he touched his lips to hers again, it was light and easy. And brief—for both their sakes.

"Good night, Zoe."

Chapter Nine

Zoe sat cross-legged on the rosewood sofa in the parlor, hip-deep in samples, trying to select ceramic tiles and grout colors for the upstairs bathrooms. Beside her were strewn catalogs offering fixtures and hardware for the cabinets, stacks of paint chips and wallpaper books. Overhead, everything was quiet, and the silence was distracting.

She'd grown used to the sounds of construction—the shuffle and stomp of the workers' boots across the floors, the harsh bark of their gruff voices, the buzz of saws, the hum of sanders, the pound of hammers. It was unbelievably noisy and incredibly chaotic, but she loved to listen to the sounds of work in progress and she was pleased with the progress that had been made.

Today, however, was Saturday, and Tyler's crew had the day off. Everyone except Tyler, of course, who had come by to finish taping and mudding the drywall in the attic.

She heard his footsteps on the stairs, then the slap of the screen door against its frame as he went back out to his truck for one thing or another. She turned her attention back to the samples and sighed.

When she heard the door again and glanced up to see Tyler coming into the room, she smiled. "How are things going upstairs?"

"I'm making progress," he told her, then raised an eyebrow as he took in the books and papers strewn around her. "How about you?"

"Not much," she admitted. "After a few hours staring at color samples, champagne and seashell are starting to look the same."

"Ready to throw in the towel and run off to Hawaii with me?" he asked. "We could dance around in grass skirts, drink rum punch out of coconut shells, make love on the beach with the waves lapping at our toes and sleep snuggled together under the stars."

She smiled. "As tempting as that sounds right now, I have to say 'no.'"

"I'd go—but only for the sleeping under the stars part," Jessica Armstrong piped in from behind him. "Heck, I'd do anything for a solid three hours of shut-eye."

"And I'd take you," Tyler said. "If I didn't think that your husband would hunt me down and kill me."

"I'm glad I found out about your fickle affections before I accepted your offer," Zoe told him.

"You'd already turned me down," he reminded her. "I was merely trying to mend my broken heart in the arms of another beautiful woman."

Zoe couldn't help but laugh at the ready response. "Smooth as glass—and just as slippery."

"Speaking of beautiful women..." Tyler scooped the baby from Jessica's arms, held her high. "Are you keeping Mommy up at night?"

Libby answered his question with a wide toothless smile.

"Day *and* night," Jess clarified.

"This little angel?" He grinned at Jess before turning his attention to Zoe. "By the way, I was supposed to let you know that Jessica and Libby are here."

"Thanks."

"We were just on our way home from Libby's checkup, and I thought we'd stop in to see how the house is coming along," Jessica said. "But if this is a bad time..."

She shook her head. "This is a great time."

"That's because Zoe likes to procrastinate," Tyler said.

"And what are you doing right now?"

"Doing what he does best," Jessica interjected. "Flirting with the ladies."

He shrugged, grinned. "We all have our strengths."

"Give me my baby and get back to work."

He touched his lips gently to Libby's forehead before passing her over. "We'll be ready to grout by the end of the week," he told Zoe. "Unless you change your mind about Hawaii."

"I'll have the colors picked by Wednesday."

He nodded, already on his way out the door.

Jessica shook her head as she watched him go. "If he wasn't so darn sweet, that charm of his could be dangerous."

"I imagine that charm *will* be dangerous if he ever focuses it on one woman."

"Like the way his brother focused on you?" Jessica teased.

Zoe decided to let that question pass as she untangled her legs and pushed herself to her feet. "Can I get you a drink? I've got iced tea or lemonade."

"Lemonade sounds great," Jess said. "I've been trying to cut down on my caffeine intake while I'm nursing—it seems like the smallest amount winds Libby up like that bunny in the battery commercials."

Zoe chuckled at the image. "Did you want to come into the kitchen or—"

"Yes, please," Jessica said quickly. "I heard Mason telling Nick about the kitchen renovation and I'd love to see it."

"Well, let's have that drink, then I'll give you the grand tour if you want."

"Sounds great."

While Jessica sipped her drink, Zoe stole a cuddle with the baby.

"She's so beautiful," she said, just a little wistfully.

"She is, isn't she? I know I'm probably biased because she's mine, but after wanting a baby for so long, I look at her and think she's just perfect."

"Even when she's screaming at 3:00 a.m.?"

Jessica laughed. "Even when I feel like screaming right along with her. I just remind myself that we waited more than eighteen years to experience midnight feedings and dirty diapers."

"Eighteen years?" Zoe asked, surprised.

"Yeah. It's a long story but one that finally has a happy ending—or happy beginning, as I like to think of it since our life together has really just begun."

"I like the idea of a happy beginning—and to think that's what I'm working toward here."

"In Pinehurst? Or specifically with the house?"

"Both," she admitted.

"And Mason?" Jessica asked. "Where does he fit into your plans?"

"He doesn't. Didn't. I mean, he wasn't supposed to. Now…I just don't know."

The other woman chuckled. "I actually think I know what you mean, because that's exactly how I felt when Nick came back into my life and turned everything upside down. It's a wonderfully terrifying feeling, isn't it?"

"More terrifying than wonderful sometimes," she said.

"He's a great guy," Jessica said.

"But?"

"But nothing. I just happen to think he's terrific."

"Oh. I thought that was your prelude to the same warning everyone else has given me—that he'll break my heart if I let him."

Jessica looked genuinely startled. "If anything, I was going to ask you to tread gently so you don't trample on his."

"I don't think there's any worry about that."

"Then you obviously haven't noticed the way he looks at you."

"There's…an attraction," Zoe admitted. "I'm aware of that."

"He's a lot more than attracted," Jessica said. "He's at least halfway in love with you."

She shook her head. "No. Neither one of us is looking for any kind of deep emotional involvement."

Jessica smiled. "One of the lessons I learned over the years is that life doesn't always follow the path we want it to. I also learned that the twists and turns can sometimes lead us in a direction we never knew we wanted to go."

"Speaking of direction," Zoe said, in a not-too-subtle attempt to change the topic. "We should head upstairs to start our tour of the house."

They chatted about the renovations as they moved from the attic back down to the kitchen, then continued their conversation while an enthusiastic Libby banged a spoon on the glass-tiled countertop Zoe had opted for over granite after seeing something similar on a home decorating show.

"You've certainly been busy in the past few months," Jessica noted.

"I've done a lot of cleaning, painting and gardening, but not much else," Zoe admitted. "Tyler and his crew have been doing the major renovating."

"I love these tiles," Jessica said. "You obviously have good instincts about what works—or maybe just really great taste."

"I've done a lot of research," Zoe admitted. "Trying

to balance the traditional style of the house with modern conveniences and contemporary designs."

"Your photography background must have helped, too, letting you see things from different angles, knowing what to focus on and what to fade out."

She shrugged. "I never really thought about that."

"It's probably so instinctive now that you wouldn't need to."

"Maybe."

"I really did want a tour of the house," Jessica said. "But that's not the only reason I stopped by."

Zoe went to the refrigerator for the pitcher of lemonade to refill their glasses. As she did so, the other woman reached into her diaper bag and pulled out an envelope of photographs.

"I finished off a roll of film at Mason's barbecue and finally got around to getting the pictures developed," she said. "But there were several photos that I don't remember taking—that I couldn't have taken."

Zoe felt her heart pounding in her chest as Jess opened the envelope, racing as she flipped through the photos until she got to the ones she'd been referring to. She spread a half-dozen shots on the countertop—two of Jessica smiling down at the baby latched onto her breast, two close-ups of the baby nursing, then one of Jessica holding the baby against her shoulder, and another of her pressing her lips to the baby's forehead.

They were good photos, Zoe thought objectively. The lighting and angle and composition confirming that the photographer had at least a certain amount of talent.

"Did you take them?" Jessica asked.

She nodded. "I didn't mean to intrude. I was walking past while you were feeding Libby, and it was such a beautiful image and the camera was right there. I just couldn't resist."

"Please don't apologize. The pictures are fabulous," Jessica said. "I remember Mason mentioning that you were a fashion photographer in New York, but I had no idea you were this good. I mean, Libby's pretty darn cute, but these pictures are phenomenal. So good, in fact, I was hoping you might be willing to take some more."

"I don't really take pictures anymore."

The other woman laughed. "Could have fooled me."

"I mean professionally," she said. "I haven't worked as a photographer in almost two years, and until a few weeks ago, I hadn't even picked up a camera in that time."

"I don't know why you gave up your career—and it's none of my business," Jessica said. "But if you've started taking pictures again, maybe it's because you want to."

It was something she'd wondered herself, and she'd realized that her willingness to pick up a camera again was a definite sign of healing.

"I'm not trying to pressure you. I'm just asking you to think about it."

"I will," she promised.

Over the next few days, Zoe thought about it a lot. And because the pictures of Jessica and Libby had turned out so well, she finally found the courage to take the four rolls of film from Claire's camera into the photo-finishing center at the drugstore. When she picked them up a couple hours later, she was pleasantly surprised by the quality of those pictures, too.

Just looking at the photos of the baby birds, she could hear those frantic peeps that had drawn her attention from her gardening to the discovery of the nest. There were pictures of Rosie, too—more than she remembered taking. But the images made her smile at the memory of the dog's crazy antics, the way he'd alternately barked at and cowered from the mother bird, who would swoop down at him to draw him away from the location of her nest and her babies.

And finally, pictures of the house. Most of the earlier shots had been taken by Claire, and she was grateful to her friend for that. Recently, she'd been so focused on all the work still to be done that she hadn't realized how much work had been accomplished until she looked at those "before" photos. Seeing them now, she finally understood how far she had come—not just with respect to the renovations of the house but in every aspect of her life.

She'd survived the break-up of her marriage, the loss of her job, the move out of Manhattan. She was building a new life now—a good life—and she wasn't going to let old fears and insecurities hold her back any longer.

When she got home from the drugstore, she called Jessica and told her she'd take the pictures of Libby.

Then she called Mason and invited him for dinner.

When Mason accepted Zoe's invitation, he was looking forward to a few hours in her company and a good meal. When he showed up at her house at the appointed hour, there was a red sauce simmering on the stove, the tangy scents of tomato and garlic in the air, an open bottle of merlot on the table and tall slender candles in fancy glass holders.

He was touched that she would go to so much trouble and, recognizing that the scene had been set for seduction, grateful that the wait was almost, finally, over.

"Smells good," he said, leaning close to sniff as she stirred the sauce.

"Thanks." She smiled, but he could see a hint of nerves around the edges.

He wanted to turn off the stove, take her in his arms and take her upstairs to bed, but he knew the nerves were evidence of both apprehension and anticipation. He took a step back, reminding himself that he'd waited two months already, another hour or so wouldn't make a difference—except to Zoe. And he very much wanted everything to be right for Zoe.

He knew she hadn't been with anyone since her husband, and after the end of a nine-year marriage, he could understand that she'd be a little nervous about being intimate with someone else. He was flattered that she'd chosen him to be that someone else—and determined that he wouldn't disappoint her.

"Can I pour the wine?" he asked.

"Yes. Please." She put the lid back on the sauce, then turned up the burner under the pot of water she'd set to boil.

He poured and offered her a glass.

Her hand was trembling, just a little, when she took it from him. He didn't mind that she was nervous—

heck, he was nervous, too—but he didn't want her to be afraid, and he wasn't convinced that she wasn't both.

She sipped the wine. Then sipped again, as if hoping the alcohol would help settle her nerves. As tightly as she was wound, he figured she'd be intoxicated before she was relaxed. So he took the glass from her fingers and set it on the counter.

"Let's try something else," he said.

She read the intent in his eyes—knew he was going to kiss her. She was ready for it, eager even. She wanted her heart to pound the way it always did when he kissed her, the echo of it so loud in her ears that she couldn't hear herself think. Or maybe it was that the touch of his mouth on hers rendered her unable to think.

In any case, she'd been thinking about this night for too long already, carefully planning every step, rehearsing every word and movement. She didn't want to think anymore—she just wanted him to kiss her.

And he did—but the kiss wasn't quite what she'd expected. It wasn't the hot, hungry demand that caused her blood to heat and her body to melt. It was the softest whisper of his lips at her temple that made her heart sigh. Then a gentle touch to her cheek, a feather-light caress along her jaw, and—finally—a slow brush of his mouth against hers.

"More," she said, and sliding a hand around the back of his neck, pulled his head down.

He gave her more. As his lips cruised over hers, his tongue dipped in and his hands slid up. Desire pulsed like blood through her veins, a wave that rushed through her and washed away all her worries and fears.

Yes, this was what she wanted—to be swept away, to let the attraction that had been building between them for so long follow its natural course. Why had she thought to complicate it with explanations about things that couldn't possibly matter here and now? Why was she worried about what had happened in the past when the present was filled with such glorious promise?

There would be plenty of time for talking later. Much later, she hoped. For now, she just wanted Mason. She wanted to be with him in every way, to touch him and be touched by him, to feel like a woman should feel when she's with a man without all kinds of history and baggage in the way.

But as much as she wished it was possible, she couldn't will that history and baggage away. As tempted as she was to remain silent and just let things happen, she knew that wouldn't be fair to either of them.

She made herself ease back.

"We should turn off that sauce," he said.

She nodded. "Yes. No." Then shook her head. "I mean, yes. But wait," she said, when he reached for her again.

"I think we've waited long enough, don't you?"

The blatant hunger in the depths of his eyes made her heart stutter, her knees quiver.

She swallowed. "I want to be with you, Mason, more than you can imagine but…"

His hands stroked up her back. "Tell me what you're afraid of."

She closed her eyes and leaned forward against his chest, for just a minute. "I'm afraid that you'll change your mind."

His laugh was strained. "Why the hell would I do that?"

"Because there's something I have to tell you."

He continued to rub her back, silently waiting for her to continue.

She'd known this moment was coming, that she would have to tell him. He meant too much for her to continue to withhold something so important from him. But she'd worried about it—finding the right words, choosing the right moment.

Except that the moment had chosen her, and now words seemed to elude her.

She pulled out of his arms and took a step back, needing to face him, to see him, when she spoke.

He was watching her—steadily, patiently. Waiting, as he'd been waiting for weeks already. He was her neighbor, her friend, and she hoped he might soon be her lover. But first she had to trust him with the truth she'd been hiding.

She drew in a deep breath, linked her hands together, and said the words she'd never spoken aloud to anyone before, "I'm a breast cancer survivor."

He stared at her, his face pale, his eyes blank—as if he didn't understand the words she'd said or didn't believe them.

"What—" he swallowed. "How—"

It wasn't quite the reaction she'd hoped for, though she'd known he would be surprised by her revelation. She'd never hinted at what she'd been through, had deliberately kept the details to herself. She'd never felt comfortable sporting pink ribbons or talking about her diagnosis or treatment. In fact, she could count on one hand the number of people she'd told about her experience because she believed it was no one else's business—until she decided to share her surgically altered body with someone else.

So she could understand why Mason was looking a little shell-shocked by her announcement.

"I was diagnosed in August, two years ago. I had a—" she drew in a breath "—a mastectomy. And reconstructive surgery. That was in September."

She was surprised she'd managed to summarize the angst and fear that had plagued her for so long in so few words, but she didn't want to rehash the details, didn't want to relive the terror. She didn't want Mason to think about what she'd been through except to help him understand that these events had brought her to where she was now.

"The follow-up tests and check-ups have been normal," she continued, in an effort to reassure both of them.

Mason still didn't say anything, and his continued silence made her uneasy.

But she covered her discomfort with a shrug. "Anyway, I thought you should know."

The words buzzed in Mason's head like swarming cicadas. Words he would never have anticipated, could never have guessed.

breastcancerbreastcancerbreastcancer

No—it couldn't be true. Fate couldn't be that cruel. Not to Zoe—beautiful, sweet, amazing Zoe.

He barely heard anything she said after those two words.

And she was looking at him now, watching him, waiting for him to say something.

He swallowed.

Jesus, what did she want him to say? How the hell was he supposed to respond to something like that?

All he could say was, "I'm sorry."

Blindly, he stumbled out the door.

Chapter Ten

Zoe knew there was no point in feeling hurt or angry, but her emotions were stronger than reason, and she was both. She was hurt that Mason had walked out without a backward glance, angry that the relationship they'd been building didn't mean enough to him to want to at least try to work it out, and angrier at herself for letting it matter.

Because she couldn't deny that it did matter—not when the tears were already spilling onto her cheeks.

And as she sank to the floor, her eyes fixed on the door through which he'd made his hasty escape, she felt as if her heart was splitting wide open.

She didn't know how long she sat there or how long she cried before the tears finally stopped. When they did, she wiped the wetness from her cheeks and pushed herself to her feet. Though her throat ached and her eyes burned, she refused to wallow in self-pity any longer. She would channel her energies in a more productive direction, she decided, and started to paint.

She was finishing up the trim in The Rose Room—the name she'd given to the room at the southwest corner of the second floor since it had a narrow balcony that overlooked the rose gardens—when the doorbell rang. A quick glance at her watch revealed that it was almost midnight, and she tried to remember if she'd locked the door after Mason had gone. And then she wondered if maybe he'd come back, and she nearly tripped down the stairs in her haste to get to the door.

But it wasn't Mason at the door—it was Claire.

And she cursed herself for the twinge of disappointment even as she forced a smile and opened the door. "Isn't it a little late for an I-was-in-the-neighborhood-and-thought-I'd-drop-by visit?"

"It's actually an I-was-on-my-way-home-from-night-class-and-saw-your-lights-blazing-and-wondered-what-the-heck-was-going-on visit."

"Well, it's kind of hard to paint in the dark," Zoe explained.

"I'm sure it is," her friend agreed. "But why are you painting at midnight?"

She shrugged. "I wasn't feeling very tired, so I thought I might as well do something productive."

"At midnight?" Claire said again.

"I've actually been at it a little while. And I should get back—before my brush dries out."

"Mind if I come up and take a look?"

"Of course not." Zoe headed toward the wide stairs in the middle of the foyer. "You'll be amazed by how much has changed since you were here last."

"You're pleased with the progress, then?"

"Yeah. Tyler knows I'm anxious to have everything ready so I can start advertising after Christmas for a spring opening, so he's had his crew putting in overtime whenever they can."

"What about Tyler's brother?"

Zoe carefully scraped the excess paint from the bristles. "Mason? What about him?"

"I just wondered how things were going there," Claire said.

She continued to paint, slowly, deliberately. "Things aren't going anywhere with Mason."

"Oh."

She didn't have to look at her friend to know that she was frowning—and waiting for more of an explanation than the one Zoe had just given her. But Zoe didn't know what else to say.

"When I saw the two of you together at the barbecue, it seemed like you were definitely moving forward."

"Well, that was before."

Though she'd been certain she'd already cried all of the tears she had in her, she felt the telltale sting as her eyes filled again and quickly averted her gaze so Claire wouldn't see this evidence of her distress.

"You told him about your cancer," her friend guessed.

"Yes, I told him. Tonight, in fact." She tried to sound

casual but couldn't hide the raw anguish in her voice. "Because I thought we were moving forward and that he had a right to know before we did."

"I'm sorry, Zoe."

She shrugged. "So am I, but I can't change the way he feels."

"Maybe not," Claire agreed. "But what about your feelings?"

"I'm hurt—and angry. And there's a part of me that just wants to sit down and cry." She managed a teary smile. "But the truth is, I've already done that, and it seems ridiculous to cry over something like this considering that, in the past two years I lost my breast, my career, and my husband. In comparison, the end of a relationship that had barely begun to a man I didn't even know a couple of months ago should be insignificant."

"Maybe it should be," Claire said gently. "But it's not."

"No, it's not," she agreed, her attention deliberately focused on the trim she was painting.

Her friend was silent for a long moment while Zoe finished around the door. When she dipped her brush into the paint again, she saw Claire watching her.

"I'm fine now, really." She spoke the assurance knowing it wasn't true, but hoping it would be.

While Zoe was painting, Mason was trying his damnedest not to think about what she'd told him. Trying not to admit that she'd finally given him the missing piece of the puzzle he'd been trying to put together over the past few months, the piece that made all the little things he'd wondered about suddenly make sense.

The way she'd been comfortable and easy in the beginning, the first hint of nerves only starting to show when he indicated a personal interest. The way she'd kissed him back with a passion that made him ache and yearn, but pulled away from any more intimate contact.

And yet, even while the knowledge solved one puzzle it created another because he couldn't reconcile the woman he knew, the woman he'd come to care for so deeply, with her condition. She seemed so young and beautiful, so strong and vibrant, so vitally alive. But he knew the cancer would take all of that from her. It would steal the glow from her cheeks, the sparkle from her eyes and, eventually, the last breath from her body. It would eat away at her spirit and devour her soul until she was nothing more than a shell of the woman he'd come to know and admire.

He knew only too well what cancer did to a body— and to the people left behind. And he wanted no part of any of it. He refused to let himself get caught up again in what had been his worst nightmare—refused to even think about it.

Instead of thinking, he got rip-roaring drunk.

Mason was awakened Sunday morning by a rough and impatient shake.

"What the hell happened to you?"

It was Tyler's voice.

He blinked and tried to focus bleary eyes on his

brother. His gaze landed instead on the half-empty bottle of Jack Daniel's and the single glass on the table in front of him. Well, that explained why his head was pounding as if there was a little man with a sledgehammer trying to break out from the inside.

"Here." Tyler shoved a mug of hot coffee into his hand and dropped a bottle of aspirin in his lap.

Mason put the coffee aside to pry open the lid on the aspirin. Damn childproof caps.

Tyler grabbed the bottle back, popped the top and shook out four tablets.

"Thanks." Mason swallowed them down with a mouthful of hot coffee.

"Private party last night?"

"Yeah."

"Wanna tell me why?"

"No."

"Then I'll guess," Tyler said, settling into a chair with his own mug of coffee. "Zoe."

"I said I don't want to talk about it."

"I stopped by her house this morning," his brother continued anyway. "It wasn't too early, but I got her out of bed. She didn't look half as rough as you do, but it was obvious she didn't sleep last night. What happened—you two have a disagreement about what color to paint the dining room?"

"Very funny."

"Well, give me a hint, because I can't imagine why you'd want to screw up the best thing that ever happened to you."

Mason finished his coffee and pushed himself off the

couch to go for a refill. "How about finding out that Zoe has breast cancer?"

"Oh, hell." Tyler followed him into the kitchen.

"Yeah—that about sums it up."

"When did she find out? What kind of treatment is she going to need?"

He took another long swallow of coffee. "She found out two years ago. She had a mastectomy."

His brother frowned. "Then she's okay now?"

"Mom thought she was going to be okay, too, remember?"

"Of course I remember. But that was twenty years ago, and if you're using the memory of what she went through as an excuse to let go of Zoe now, then you don't deserve her, anyway."

"The cancer didn't just kill her, Tyler—it killed Dad, too."

"Did it ever occur to you that it was guilt as much as grief that made him drown himself in the bottle? Yeah, I remember what Mom went through. And I remember who was there with her in the end—you and me and Grandma. Dad couldn't handle seeing her like that, knowing he was losing her, and he wasted the last six months they might have had together by mourning her before she was gone."

"He loved her too much to watch her die."

"Did we love her any less?"

Mason frowned at that.

"Of course not," Tyler answered his own question. "And that's why you've spent the past twenty years avoiding anything that might even resemble a relationship.

Then Zoe came along, and you seemed to be building not just a house but the foundation of a future together.

"Now you have to ask yourself—why are you running scared? Are you worried that Zoe's battle with cancer might not be over and you don't have what it takes to stand by her? Or are you afraid of losing her? Because if that's your concern, well, you've pretty much ensured that all by yourself."

Zoe knew it was inevitable that she would cross paths with Mason sooner or later. They were neighbors, after all, and it wouldn't have surprised her to run into him at DiMarco's Grocery or Anderson's Hardware or Walton's Ice Cream Parlor. It did surprise her to find him standing at her back door less than forty-eight hours after making a quick escape through that same entrance.

And it annoyed her to find that his appearance there made her heart skip and race after he'd so mercilessly trampled upon it. And if she felt a small measure of satisfaction because his eyes were bloodshot and shadowed with dark circles, his jaw was unshaven and he generally looked like hell, she figured she was entitled.

"If you're looking for the beast, I haven't seen him," she told him.

"I'm not," Mason said. "I came to see you, if you've got a few minutes."

She glanced at her watch, torn between wanting him to stay and wishing he would go. "My dinner's in the oven, so I've got about ten minutes," she finally said.

"Can I come in?"

She stepped away from the door to allow him entry, but she didn't invite him to sit down or offer him a drink. Whatever his reason for being there, she didn't see any point in dragging it out. Her pride was all that she had left now, and she wasn't going to risk losing that, too, by asking for something he couldn't give her.

Instead, she moved to the counter where she'd left the lettuce when she went to answer the door, and began tearing up the leaves for a salad. She heard his footsteps follow her into the room, felt the weight of his eyes on her, but she deliberately kept her own gaze focused on her task.

"I owe you an apology," he said at last.

"You don't owe me anything, Mason."

"Yes, I do," he insisted. "And I'd appreciate it if you'd at least hear me out."

She finished her task before pushing the bowl aside and turning to face him.

"I freaked out when you said *cancer,* and I'm sorry."

She heard the words, knew he meant them, but an apology couldn't ease the ache inside. Nothing could.

"It's not an uncommon reaction," she told him. "I know a lot of people who still whisper the word, as if speaking it out loud will somehow bring the curse of the disease into their own homes."

"It just caught me off guard," he said. "I mean, you're so young, and you seem so healthy."

"I *am* healthy," she said. "I might not be whole, but I'm healthy."

He winced at that. "What you've been through doesn't make you any less beautiful or any less of a woman, Zoe."

"Are you saying it doesn't matter that I've lost a breast?" she challenged.

He couldn't meet her gaze when he said, "I'm saying that it shouldn't."

"But it does, doesn't it?"

He was silent for a long moment, then he finally said, "Yes."

It was hard to appreciate his honesty when the single word scraped at open wounds that were already raw and bleeding.

"My mother—" he had to clear his throat. "My mother died of breast cancer."

The revelation didn't shock her. She was familiar with the statistics, knew that one in every eight women would be diagnosed with breast cancer at some point in their lives. And when she'd cleared her mind enough to think beyond the fact that he'd walked out on her to wonder why, she'd suspected that he'd been close to someone who'd battled the disease. Only now did she remember him telling her about his mother's death, and his father's a few years later. She'd never thought to ask how she'd died, and it had certainly never occurred to her that his mother might have succumbed to the same disease she'd battled herself.

"I don't know the details of when or how she found the lump," he continued, "but I know that she didn't tell anyone for a long time because I remember her and my dad arguing about that. He didn't have any medical coverage through his work, so she refused to make unnecessary trips to the doctor. By the time she went to have it checked out, the cancer had spread."

His voice was level, almost detached, but she noticed that his fingers had curled around the edge of the counter, gripping it so tightly his knuckles were white. "They cut off her breast, put her through chemo and then radiation.

"Slash, poison, burn." He shook his head. "It was supposed to make her better. All it did was make the last two years of her life a living hell."

Her heart ached for him—for the teenager who'd lost his mother, and for the man still suffering over that loss. "I'm so sorry, Mason."

"When I hear the word *cancer*—I can't help remembering. And I hate to think of you going through all of that."

"I didn't," she told him. "I chose to have a mastectomy instead of a lumpectomy to reduce the need for follow-up treatment."

"My mother had a mastectomy."

"But you said her cancer had already spread," she said gently. "My doctors were confident that mine was found early enough that I didn't need to worry about involvement of the lymph nodes, and they recommended—partly because I was so young, I think—that I have only the lump removed and save the breast."

"Why didn't you?"

"Do you really want to talk about this?"

"No," he admitted. "I wish it was a completely irrelevant topic, but since it isn't, I want to know what you went through."

The timer buzzed, indicating that her dinner was ready. She turned it off and pulled her fish out of the oven. "I'm not sure that I want to talk about it."

"Maybe you should anyway," he said. "Because I'm guessing, now that I know about the cancer and when you were diagnosed, that there's a connection between everything you tried to dismiss as 'crossroads'—the breakdown of your marriage, your sudden change of career, the move to Pinehurst."

"You're right," she admitted. "My diagnosis created something of a domino effect on all areas of my life—and apparently some of the tiles are still tumbling." And if she was completely honest with herself, she'd admit that she'd lived with the secrets for so long, been so careful to keep the truth close, that she really hadn't acknowledged and accepted all of the consequences herself. Maybe telling him would be a mistake. Or maybe, in some ways, it might be cathartic.

So when he asked again why she'd chosen to have the mastectomy, she took a deep breath and answered.

"Because it seemed easier to cover up the loss of my breast than the loss of my hair." The wry smile didn't hint at the knots tangled in her belly. "I know that sounds bizarre and vain and, in retrospect, I should have considered the fact that my hair would have grown back by now—and my breast never will.

"But it was more than just losing my hair—it was the fear of being sick, of everyone knowing what I was going through. I didn't want people to see that I had cancer because…" her voice faltered. "Because then I would have to admit that I had cancer."

"You didn't tell anyone?" he asked, obviously surprised.

"Not at first. It was hard enough telling Scott. I

thought breast cancer was something that afflicted older women. I was only twenty-seven years old. I felt ashamed—as if it was somehow my fault that my body was defective. I was angry and helpless and confused. And terrified that everyone would start treating me differently.

"I just wanted to pretend everything was normal." She shook her head as she swallowed around the tightness in her throat. "No, that's not true. I wanted everything to *be* normal.

"But it wasn't. And I had to face that fact every time I picked up my camera to take pictures of women who were beautiful and perfect and whole."

"Is that the real reason you left Manhattan?"

"One of the reasons," she admitted. "I thought I could have the surgery and reconstruction and get back to work as if nothing had changed.

"Except that everything had changed. I tried to go through the motions of taking pictures, but it was a disaster. I played with lenses, adjusted angles, checked lighting, clicked the shutter. By all outward appearances, I was doing the job as I'd always done the job. But when I looked at the contact sheets, I saw that I'd only been focusing on parts. I'd have a picture of a shoulder or a hand—not the whole model or the whole of anything I was supposed to be photographing.

"Scott tried to be understanding, but he was caught between his editorial responsibilities and his messed-up wife. The magazine had to bring in another photographer and redo the whole shoot, which threw off the entire production schedule, cost a ton of money and raised a lot of questions about my ability to fulfill the terms of my contract. So I left. It seemed like the best solution for everyone."

She pushed off the thoughts, the regrets.

It hadn't been an easy decision, but it was the decision she'd made and the one she'd live with—hopefully, for a very long time.

"Is that when your marriage fell apart?"

She shook her head. "My medical problems only made me realize how far apart we'd grown. We were two people sharing a home and a bed but essentially living separate lives. I'd always been strong and independent, and suddenly I was weak and needy—and the change scared both of us."

So many emotions coursed through him as he listened to her talk. Empathy and admiration. Concern and regret. Fear and anger.

It was the anger that seemed easiest to focus on, and he heard the evidence of it in his voice when he said, "I can't believe you're making excuses for him."

"Some people just can't cope with personal crises."

He frowned at that. "Are we still talking about your ex?"

"Yes," she said. "But I don't blame you for walking out, either. I shouldn't have let things go as far as they did without making you aware of the situation."

"And that's it?" he demanded, unaccountably annoyed by her easy capitulation. "You're just going to accept that I couldn't handle what you went through?"

She glanced away, but not before he caught a

glimpse of the tears that filled her eyes. "What do you think I should do—take off my clothes and make you look at my scars?"

"I don't know," he said, though there was a part of him that almost wished she would. He wanted her to force the issue, to push him for more than he was ready to give, because then he could blame her for things not working out.

"I'm pretty sure that display wouldn't make either one of us feel any better," she told him.

"I really am sorry…for everything you went through."

She shrugged. "Now you know the whole story."

"Except where we go from here," he said softly, surprising himself as much as he'd obviously surprised Zoe with the words.

When he'd come here tonight, he'd done so because he'd wanted to apologize. And because he'd needed her to understand why it was impossible for their relationship to develop any further. But as he opened up to her about his past and listened to her talk about her experience, he found himself wondering if a future with Zoe really was impossible.

The hope that flared briefly in her eyes in response to his statement was quickly eclipsed by wariness, as if she didn't dare let herself hope, as if she wouldn't risk trusting in him again. "Where do you want to go?"

He stared at her for a long moment, the same uncertainty he'd heard in her voice reflected in his own heart. Despite his doubts and fears, he still wanted Zoe. But there was so much at stake—more than he'd ever been willing to risk with anyone before, maybe more than he was ready to risk even now. He was trapped by his own indecision, unable to take the next step forward, yet unwilling to let her go.

"I don't know," he admitted.

She turned away to get a plate from the cupboard, clearly intent on moving ahead with her dinner plans and effectively dismissing him. "When you figure it out, you can let me know."

Chapter Eleven

Zoe was painting the gazebo when Tyler tracked her down Friday morning.

"You've been making yourself scarce this week," he noted.

"I've been up and out early every day, scouring antique stores within a hundred-mile radius in search of bookcases for the library."

"Since you're home today, I'd guess you either found what you wanted or you ran out of stores."

She smiled. "I found a gorgeous solid walnut East-lake bookcase in three sections. It's going to be delivered this afternoon."

"What time?"

"Between two and four."

"Then we'll definitely be able to make the movie."

"What movie?"

"The one we're going to see tonight."

"Thanks, Ty, but I'm not—"

"Don't say 'no,'" he urged. "It's a new sci-fi flick that I really want to see, but I hate going to the theater by myself like some loser who can't get a date."

"I don't think you'd have any trouble getting a date if you really wanted one," she said.

"Seems to me I'm having trouble right now."

"Sci-fi movies aren't really my thing."

"It's got to be better than sitting at home and brooding about the idiocy of other men."

She sighed. "I know you think your brother broke my heart, but he didn't. And even if he did, it's not your job to pick up the pieces."

"This has nothing to do with my brother," he assured her. "It has to do with me wanting to see a movie with you."

She didn't believe him for a minute, but she appreciated his effort.

"Okay," she finally agreed. "But only if you let me buy the popcorn."

Despite her initial reluctance, Zoe did enjoy the movie. And she enjoyed Tyler's company. He was handsome and charming and fun to be with, and when he said he was hungry after the movie, they picked up pasta from Mama Leone's and took it back to her house.

"I really do love the new look of the kitchen," Tyler said as he unpacked the bag of food. "I would have thought you'd put in a whole new set of cabinets if I hadn't seen you painting them myself."

"I'm not sure it's a job I'd ever want to tackle again, but I'm pleased with the way they turned out. I'm even happier with the changes you can't see—the roll-outs and dividers that help keep everything in its proper place inside the cabinets."

"Yeah, I can see you like things organized," he said, looking through the spice rack that had been attached to the inside of a cupboard door for the chili peppers. "Your spices are actually alphabetized."

"It makes it easier to find whatever I'm looking for."

He picked up a bottle, frowned at the label before putting it back. "What do you use cumin for?"

"Chili."

"One of my all-time favorites." He'd found the peppers and sprinkled a generous amount on top of his rigatoni. "There's nothing like hot chili on a cold winter day. Now if you told me you made lamb stew, too, I'd have to marry you."

"Then you're safe." Zoe twirled her fork in her angel hair pasta. "I've never cooked lamb in any shape or form. I do, however, make a pretty decent Guinness stew."

"Good enough." He reached across the table for her hand. "Wanna get hitched?"

She smiled, shaking her head, and tugged her hand away. "Been there, done that."

He suddenly turned serious. "You don't think you'll ever get married again?"

"I don't know what will happen in the future, but

right now, I can't imagine ever opening up my heart to someone that completely again."

"Except that you did, didn't you? You fell in love with my brother."

"I don't know." She toyed with her pasta. "I think I was definitely headed that way, but then there was an unexpected fork in the road."

"And my brother veered off in the wrong direction."

"He took the one that was right for him."

"What about what's right for you?"

"I'm still figuring that out myself," she said. "But I do know that I don't want to be with someone who can't accept me for who I am. I deserve better than that."

"You do," he agreed. "You're an amazing woman, Zoe. And my brother's an idiot."

She pushed away from the table to take her half-empty plate to the counter—and nearly dumped her leftovers down her front when a shadow at the back door made her jump.

She pressed a hand to her pounding heart. "Go home," she spoke to Rosie through the screen.

The dog whined.

Tyler carried his empty plate to the sink. "How did he get here?"

"The same way he always does, I guess."

"Always?"

She shrugged as she scraped the rest of her pasta back into the take-out container to go into the fridge. "It seems like always. Every day this week, that's for sure.

Usually I just tell him to go home and he goes, but last night, I had to call your brother to come and get him."

"Maybe the dog's trying to get the two of you back together."

She rolled her eyes at that.

"So what happened when you called Mason?" he asked.

"He came and got the beast."

"And?"

"And nothing. There was no reason for me to go outside and no reason for him to come in."

Tyler sighed. "Have I mentioned that my brother's an idiot?"

She smiled. "He has to figure out what he wants on his own."

Outside, Rosie barked.

Zoe pushed open the door and stepped out onto the porch. "You know your own way," she said to the animal. "Now go."

Rosie barked again.

"I'll take him over," Tyler offered.

"You don't mind?"

"Of course not. It's probably time I was heading out anyway."

She walked around to the front of the house with him. When they got to the steps, he leaned down to drop a friendly kiss on Zoe's forehead, chuckling again when he heard Rosie's whine turn to a growl.

"I'm not making any moves on her," he assured the dog. "Just saying good night."

She smiled. "Good night, Tyler. And thanks again for the movie."

"Anytime." He started to step off the porch when the crunch of tires on gravel indicated another visitor coming up the driveway.

"Expecting company?"

She shook her head as she watched the other vehicle pull up alongside Tyler's truck. It was a sportscar of some type, she guessed, with distinctively shaped head-lights low to the ground. Maybe a Porsche 911 like Scott drove.

Then the driver's side door opened and he stepped out.

"Someone you know?" Tyler asked.

"My ex-husband."

He frowned. "Do you want me to hang around?"

She smiled at that, touched by his protectiveness toward her. She was disappointed that things hadn't worked out with Mason, but she was pleased with the friendship she'd established with his brother and she'd always be grateful to Mason for that.

"Thank you." She gave him a quick hug. "But I can handle Scott."

"I'll see you tomorrow, then," he said, and led Rosie away.

Mason wasn't in the mood for company, so when he heard the brisk knock on the door, he ignored it. When the door opened and his brother walked in, he intended to ignore him, too. Until he saw that Rosie was with him.

"Where did you find him?" he asked reluctantly.

"On Zoe's porch."

The response didn't surprise him. It seemed like every time he turned around lately, the dog was at Zoe's. "Keep it up and I will put you on a leash."

Rosie growled.

"I think man's best friend has gone over to the other side," Tyler said, amusement evident in his tone. "He growled at me like that, too, when I kissed Zoe good-night."

Mason turned his scowl on his brother. "I expected that you, knowing what she's been through, would have enough sense not to play with her emotions."

Tyler arched an eyebrow, but all he said was, "I happen to care about Zoe. And, for some inexplicable reason, I care about you, too, even if you deserve to be kicked in the butt for letting her get away."

"I'm not getting into this with you again."

His brother shrugged. "Okay—I thought you might want to know that Zoe's ex-husband is back in the picture, but if you're happy with the way things are, it doesn't really matter."

"What do you mean, her ex is in the picture?"

"He showed up at her house while I was there."

"What did he want?"

"I didn't hang around to chat," Tyler said dryly.

"You left—and left Zoe alone with him?"

"He's not an escaped convict—he's her ex-husband," his brother pointed out reasonably.

But Mason wasn't in the mood to be reasonable. "Who bailed on her because he couldn't handle the consequences of her condition."

"You mean—like you did?"

Mason glowered at his brother. "It's hardly the same thing."

Tyler's only response was to raise his eyebrows.

It was Tuesday before Mason found out, again through Tyler, why Zoe's ex-husband had come to see her, and Wednesday when he agreed to try to re-open the lines of communication with her. Although he found himself second-guessing that decision every step of the way toward her house late Wednesday afternoon.

He couldn't believe he'd let his brother talk him into this ridiculous plan that Zoe would no doubt see right through. But even knowing that, he was grateful for the excuse—any excuse—to see her again. Because in the ten days that had passed since he'd walked out of her kitchen, he'd finally realized that the possibility of losing her at some unforeseeable time in the future was preferable to losing her now because he wasn't smart enough to hold on to her.

She was obviously surprised to see him, even more surprised when he revealed the reason for his visit.

"You want to borrow some cumin?"

"Two tablespoons," he said.

"Okay." But she was frowning as she pulled open the cupboard door. "What do you need it for?"

"Tyler's making chili."

"Your brother's cooking?"

Mason nodded. "He was chopping up peppers and onions and stuff, so he asked me to come over to see if you had the cumin."

Zoe handed him a bottle. "There you go."

"Thanks."

"Was there something else you needed?" she asked, when he made no move to leave.

"No." He turned away, then back again. "Yes."

She waited.

"Tyler told me that your ex-husband offered you a job."

"Not a permanent position," she said. "Just as a fill-in for one shoot."

"Are you going to do it?" he wanted to know.

"He's stuck—the photographer that he'd planned to use was double-booked, and it would be a logistical nightmare to reschedule the whole thing."

"And you believe that this other photographer was suddenly unavailable?"

"I can't imagine that Scott would have come to me otherwise."

"Maybe he wants you back and figures if he can get you taking pictures for the magazine again, you might realize you've missed it and decide to return to Manhattan."

"I have no reason to question his motives," she told him, wondering why Mason was doing so and why her decision even mattered to him. "And this is a good opportunity for me—not to mention a potentially lucrative one."

"And after the photo shoot is finished?"

"I'll come back."

"When will that be?"

She shrugged. "Probably in four or five days."

"Four or five days taking pictures?"

"The photo shoot should only take a day or two, depending on the weather, then add another day on each end to accommodate the travel."

"It doesn't take more than a couple of hours to drive to New York City."

"No," she agreed. "But it takes a little longer to get to Exuma."

"Exuma?" he echoed dubiously.

"That's where the photo shoot is scheduled."

He scowled. "You're going to the Bahamas with your ex-husband?"

"I'm going to the Bahamas with the magazine."

"Is your ex-husband going to be there?"

"Why are you doing this?" she asked wearily. "You were the one who decided you didn't want me, remember?"

"I never said I didn't want you."

"You're right—you never said those words." Her eyes glittered with tears. "I read between the lines when you ran out the door."

The sharpness in her tone wasn't unexpected—the tears were. He deserved her anger, was prepared to deal with that. It was the hurt underlying the temper that cut him at the knees. He'd never wanted to hurt her, had never realized how much damage he could do to her heart in trying to protect his own.

"You read wrong," he said.

"It doesn't matter," she told him. "You got what you came here for and I have to pack."

As he watched her turn away, panic reared up like a wild beast, kicking and clawing and tearing him up inside. He couldn't let her go—not with so much still unresolved between them.

"Dammit, Zoe." He grabbed her arm, spun her back toward him. "If I didn't want you, this would be easy."

Her eyes flashed fire as she opened her mouth to respond, no doubt to tell him it was too little too late. He didn't want to hear it. He didn't need her to tell him that he'd been an idiot. What he needed right now was Zoe.

He hauled her against him and covered her mouth with his.

Her eyes widened with shock, her body stiffened. But she didn't pull away. And as his lips moved over hers, he felt the tension slowly begin to seep away until, finally, her eyes closed, her lips softened and her body melted against his.

He wrapped his arms around her, drawing her close, closer.

Beautiful, sweet Zoe.

He didn't know if he murmured the words against her lips or just inside his head. It didn't matter, really. What mattered was her response. The soft moan that came from deep in her throat as she fisted her hands in his hair and parted her lips for the searching thrust of his tongue.

He could feel the pounding of her heart, the frantic beat that matched his own.

Want you. So much.

His hands slid down her back, over the sweet curve of her buttocks. Desire—hot and greedy—surged through him.

He wanted to touch and taste and take.

He wanted to make her tremble and sigh. He wanted to feel her shudder and hear her moan. He wanted her breathless and quivering, aching for him as he ached for her. Then he wanted to tear away her clothes and bury himself in the sweet heat of her body.

The fantasy of doing just that—right here and right now—was shockingly vivid in his mind, the ache in his body painfully real.

He fought to remember that as much as he wanted her, he didn't want it to be like this. Not with so many questions and doubts still between them.

So instead of tearing away her clothes, he tore his mouth from hers.

His kiss had surprised Zoe, which was why his withdrawal only infuriated her more. She'd been on an emotional roller coaster for the past week-and-a-half, and every time she thought things were starting to level out, he sent her flying again.

"Damn you, Mason." She slapped her hands against his chest as if to push him away. She *should* push him away—make it clear that she wasn't going to let him churn her up and then walk out on her again. But somehow, instead of pushing him away, her fingers curled into his shirt and pulled him closer.

This time, it was her mouth that found his. This time, it was her lips and teeth and tongue that snapped the tight rein on his passion.

With a growl of pent-up frustration, he pulled her close, banding his arms around her to hold her against his hot, hard and very aroused body.

She thought she'd resigned herself to the fact that she and Mason would never be lovers. She couldn't have imagined that their relationship would be able to move forward after he'd walked out on her. But somehow he was here, wanting her, and making her want him.

If she let herself think about it, she might find herself filled with doubts and fears and insecurities. So she refused to think about it. The how or why didn't matter—not right now. All that mattered was that she felt more alive in this moment, in his arms, than she'd felt in a very long time.

She wound her arms around his neck. "You're not walking out on me this time."

"No." His kiss was long and deep. "I'm not going anywhere."

She moaned with anticipation as those fast, eager hands traced her curves through the thin barrier of her clothing, then gasped with pleasure when they found the warm flesh beneath.

But she wanted to touch as much as be touched. Despite shaking fingers, she managed to unfasten the buttons that ran down the front of his shirt. She pushed the material aside and let her palms slide over all that smooth taut skin, her fingers tracing the contours of all those hard, rippling muscles.

She touched her lips to his chest and inhaled the tangy masculine scent that made her want to gobble him up in quick, greedy bites. The temptation was more than she could resist, and she nipped at his shoulder, the gentle bite earning a quick, startled oath that became a tortured groan when she soothed the spot with her tongue.

"Bedroom," he muttered, scooping her into his arms. "Before I forget where we are and take you on the kitchen floor."

He took the stairs two at a time and was kicking open the bedroom door before she could catch her breath.

"Now." He lowered her gently to her feet. "Where were we?"

"Right about here," she said, tugging open the button at the top of his jeans with a quick flick of her wrist. "And here." She rubbed her palm against the hard length of him through the denim.

"I, uh—"

She had the pleasure of watching his eyes start to glaze before he circled her wrist with his fingers and tugged her hand away.

"I think you're, uh, skipping ahead a little."

"You said you wanted me," she reminded him.

"I do." His eyes were dark, intense. "More than you could imagine."

She took his hand and drew him toward the bed. "Show me."

He captured her mouth in another kiss as he eased her down onto the mattress. She wrapped herself around him, glorying in the weight of his body pressing against hers, the hardness of his arousal between her thighs.

His hands were relentless now, teasing, testing, taking, as they raced over her skin. His lips were hot and wild, scorching everywhere they touched. Desire thrummed through her with every beat of her heart, every pulse of her blood. She couldn't move, couldn't think, she could only feel.

Heat.

Want.

Need.

His hands were under her skirt now, stripping away her panties. Then his fingers gliding over her skin. From ankles to knees, knees to thighs. Her muscles quivered, her breath caught.

Then he touched her, just a feather light stroke of his fingers over the dewy curls at her center. She gasped as those fingers dipped into her. He groaned in appreciation when he found her wet and ready.

"Now," she said, her body aching for the fulfillment of joining with his.

He left her only long enough to get rid of his jeans and briefs, then took another moment to protect her before lowering himself over her again.

"Now," he agreed, and filled her.

Her eyes widened with shocked surprise at the first thrust, then closed again in dreamy delirium as he started to move inside her.

She felt the thundering beat of his heart against hers, steady and strong, when she wrapped her arms around him. She tasted the salty flavor of his skin when she pressed her lips to his throat. And she smiled in pure feminine satisfaction when the light scrape of her nails over his skin made him shudder.

They rolled over the mattress, mouths mating, hands grasping, hearts pounding. She rose up over him, her knees tight against his hips as she rode him to that dark, dangerous edge—and over.

Everything inside her that had tightened and tensed

finally burst free. When her body quivered, shuddered and slid bonelessly against him, he flipped her onto her back and drove her on.

"More," he said.

She'd thought she was spent, that there couldn't possibly be any more than the pleasure he'd already given her. Even as her mind spun and her senses shattered, she was arching beneath him.

He yanked her hips high, drove hard, harder. She hooked her legs around his waist, pulled him deep, deeper. Then they were racing together, fast, faster.

The climax tore a scream from her throat as it ripped through her, leaving her shuddering helplessly beneath the weight of his body as he groaned and emptied himself into her.

As often as Mason had imagined making love with Zoe—and over the past couple of months, he'd imagined it often—he'd never suspected that the experience would leave him feeling simultaneously drained and energized. He wanted to tuck her close to his body and curl up to sleep for a week. And he wanted her all over again.

But she apparently had other plans, because she climbed out of the bed, straightened the skirt that had bunched around her waist and tugged down the hem of her shirt.

And while he'd never been accused of being particularly insightful when it came to the methods and moods of women, he knew that something was definitely wrong.

"Zo?"

She was tugging open the drawers of her dresser, pulling out items of clothing seemingly at random. "I have to catch a plane in a few hours," she explained, "and I haven't even packed."

Her casual response and easy dismissal of the intimacy they'd just shared hit him with the force of a physical blow.

"And that's it? You're just going to leave?"

"I told you that I had to go."

"Can you at least take a later flight?"

She shook her head. "Not if I'm going to make my connection in Miami."

With a sigh of combined resignation and frustration, he scooped his jeans off the floor and pulled them on. "We need to talk about this, Zoe."

"No, we don't." She smiled at him, but he could tell it was forced. "Really, it's not a big deal."

"Not a big deal?"

"I'm not one of those women who confuse sex with love or assume that physical intimacy equals a relationship, so you don't have to worry about anything like that."

"My mistake," he said coolly.

She shoved a handful of lacy undergarments into a duffel bag. "Save the wounded act. We both got exactly what we wanted—nothing more and nothing less."

"Is that all this was to you—an opportunity to release some pent-up sexual tension?"

"I'd be a fool to think it could be anything more after you made it clear you didn't want to get involved with me," she said.

"I don't know how it is with people from New York," he said. "But where I come from, getting naked with someone usually indicates a certain level of involvement."

"But we didn't get naked, did we?"

"What?"

She shook her head. "It's okay. Really. I know my medical history makes you uncomfortable."

And suddenly the reason for her hurt and anger hit him like a two-by-four between the eyes.

"You think I didn't take your clothes off because I didn't want to look at your body?"

"It's okay," she said again. "Scott had issues with the scars, too."

"I'm not your ex-husband," he snapped. "And the only reason I didn't take your clothes off was because I was in too damn much of a hurry to get inside you. And it seemed to me that you were just as eager for the same thing."

"I really don't want to argue about this," she told him. "I'm already running behind schedule."

"Or maybe you're just running."

Her only response was to pick up her duffel bag and sling it over her shoulder.

Chapter Twelve

It was love at first sight for Zoe.

She'd had the opportunity to travel to a lot of different places when she'd worked at *Images,* but this was her first trip to Exuma and she was immediately enamored of the lush green vegetation, the crystal-clear water and the powder-soft beaches. It was, she thought, the closest thing to paradise she'd ever seen.

But as exotic and beautiful as it was, it wasn't home. And by the third day, Zoe was missing her house and wondering what Tyler's crew was working on now. Was the third-floor suite—formerly the attic—done yet? Would she be able to decorate in preparation of moving up there when she got back? Were her flowers still in bloom? Or were they uprooted because Rosie had been chasing squirrels again? Of course, thinking about Rosie made her think about Mason. Or maybe the truth was that thoughts of Mason always lingered in her mind and maybe she was missing him most of all.

She pushed those thoughts aside as she wiped perspiration from her brow with the back of her arm and waited for the models to get into position. When everything was set, she refocused the camera and snapped away until she was confident she had all the shots she needed. When she finally signaled that they were done, Scott strolled over.

She accepted the bottle of cold water with a weary smile.

"Thanks." She tipped it to her lips and drank deeply.

"Thank *you,*" he said. "You really saved my skin by coming out here."

She smiled. "You haven't seen any of the pictures yet."

"I don't need to see them to know they're great. I've been watching you enough since you got here to know you're in top form." He stroked a hand down her arm. "How does it feel—to be behind the camera again?"

"It feels good," she admitted, no longer surprised that it was true. "Except for the fact that it's nine hundred degrees in the shade." She took another long swallow, pressed the bottle to her forehead. "Whose idea was it to shoot in the Caribbean in August anyway?"

"Mine." He grinned. "I like the way you look in a bikini."

"What if I hadn't agreed to do this?"

He shrugged. "Then I would have been stuck with Perry—and he isn't half as cute in a bathing suit."

"I thought Perry was stuck in France."

"He was—is. But he expects to finish up there in another few days."

"So you could have rescheduled this shoot for next week."

He shook his head. "We had everything—including the models—booked for this week. It would have put us behind schedule and cost a fortune to delay even a few days."

"You spent a small fortune to bring me out here without even knowing if I'd be able to do the job."

"I knew you could do it—and in spectacular fashion," he said with confidence.

She smiled at that. "You never did like to admit when you'd made a mistake."

"I only ever made one," he told her. "When I signed the divorce papers."

"Our marriage was over long before that."

"Was it? I've wondered so many times since then if we could have fixed it—if maybe we still can."

"It's kind of hard to fix something that doesn't exist anymore."

"Don't you believe in second chances?"

"Sure," she said. "But I don't believe in making the same mistake a second time."

"Ouch."

She smiled. "I have a lot of good memories of the time we spent together, but I've moved on. We both have."

"You don't honestly expect me to believe you're serious about that kid you were out with the night I came to Pinehurst."

She smiled, thinking that it would have been easy to fall for Tyler—he was handsome, charming and fun. Unfortunately, she'd met his much more frustrating and complicated brother first and fallen for him, instead.

"No," she finally answered Scott's question. "Tyler and I are just friends."

"Is there someone else, then?"

She took another sip of her water as her thoughts drifted automatically to Mason. Even when he'd been trying to back off and she'd been trying to stay mad, there was an undeniable "something" that continued to draw them together—an incomprehensible chemistry that had sparked between them almost from the first and continued to build over the past couple of months until it had finally exploded in a frenzy of passion that had somehow left her both sated and yearning, both scared and wanting.

"Obviously there is someone else," he said.

"Yes, there is."

"Are you happy with him?"

"I think I could be."

"Then I hope he's a smarter man than me."

"That remains to be seen," she said lightly.

"Although he's obviously not too bright," Scott continued. "Since he let you fly off to a tropical island paradise with your ex-husband."

"He's smart enough to know he couldn't stop me," Zoe said. "And to warn me that he thought you were interested in more than my camera."

He grinned unashamedly. "Can't blame a guy for trying."

She couldn't help but smile back. "Thank you."

"For what?"

"Not giving up on me."

"I'm not going to give up hoping that you'll come back to *Images,* either."

"I can't," she said. "I'm not that person anymore."

"I know," he admitted. "The wife I loved and the photographer I admired pale in comparison to the woman you are now."

She hoped that was true. When she'd first been diagnosed, she'd thought it would be enough to survive. Now she wanted more. And in order to get "more," she needed to be a smarter, braver and stronger woman than she'd been—smart enough to recognize what she really wanted, brave enough to go after it and strong enough to fight for it.

"Thanks again for this opportunity." She kissed his cheek and turned away.

"Where are you going?" Scott demanded.

She smiled. "Home."

Zoe was tired when she got on the plane—but it was a good tired, the kind of satisfied exhaustion that came from the knowledge that she'd done her job well. The pictures would be fabulous, she was as confident as Scott about that. And though she had no intention of going back to her job at *Images,* it was both flattering and reassuring to know that she hadn't lost her touch and that there were other career options available to her if the bed-and-breakfast didn't work out the way she hoped it would.

But whatever her future might bring, she had no intention of running back to New York City. She wasn't running anywhere anymore. The girl who had taken off to college to escape the chaos of her mother's marriages, then to New York in pursuit of her husband's dreams, then away from the city and her crumbling marriage, had finally found what she hadn't realized she'd always been looking for. Maybe not with Mason—whatever their relationship might or might not be remained to be seen, but she loved the town and being close to Claire and the new friends she'd made. For the first time in her life, she truly felt as if she was home.

She stepped into the house, dropped her suitcase on the floor and kicked off her shoes. Then stared into the dining room at the neatly pressed linen cloth draped over the table, the china, crystal and silver set out for two, the candles waiting to be lit, the bottle of chardonnay chilling in a bucket of ice.

A movement by the kitchen doorway caught her eye, and when she glanced over, she saw Mason was there.

"You weren't supposed to be home until after seven."

"I caught an earlier flight. What are you doing here?"

"Making dinner." He took a few steps toward her. "How was Exuma?"

"Breathtaking. Is your stove broken?"

He smiled at that. "No. But if I'd invited you to dinner at my place, you might have said 'no.'"

And probably would have, she admitted to herself. Because as much as he'd been in her thoughts throughout her journey and despite her resolution to get in touch with him, she'd planned to wait, at least until the next day, to do so. She'd wanted to be rested and showered, dressed in something that didn't look as if she'd slept in it and wearing at least a touch of makeup. Instead, she suspected that she looked as weary as she felt, and she felt completely unprepared to see him now—especially when just looking at him made her knees weak.

"How did you get in here?"

"I borrowed my brother's key. Actually, I had to bribe him," Mason admitted. "With tickets to a baseball game."

"You gave up a ballgame to get into my house and make me dinner?"

"Not just any ballgame—the Yankees and the Red Sox." He took her hands in his. "I missed you, Zoe."

Her heart skipped, then raced. "Oh."

His smile was wry. "An I-missed-you-too would have been nice, but at least you haven't kicked me out."

She wasn't ready to put her heart on the line just yet and refused to feel guilty about it. Instead, she said, "I'm hungry, and whatever you're cooking smells good."

"Chicken Parisian with basmati rice—but it's not quite ready yet. Do you want a glass of wine while you're waiting?"

"Actually, I'd love a quick shower, if there's time."

"You've got time for a soak in the tub and the wine, if you want," he told her. "I wasn't expecting you to be early and I haven't even put the rice on yet."

"That sounds good," she agreed.

She took her wine upstairs, grateful for a few minutes to gather her thoughts and settle her emotions.

She'd wanted to see him. She couldn't deny that. But she'd expected to have a chance to prepare—to be rational and logical. It worried her that her heart had leaped so joyously at the sight of him, that his smile still had the power to make her bones melt, that she was incapable of objectivity and reason whenever he was near.

As the scented bubbles worked to soak away her fatigue, she considered whether to take a step back—or jump in with both feet.

Obviously, they had to talk about what had happened before she left and where they would go from here. She knew he cared about her, but she also knew that he had reservations about getting any more deeply involved. She couldn't blame him for that. She'd had reservations of her own long before she knew what he'd gone through with his mother.

Her heart ached when she thought of the boy he'd been—how difficult it must have been for him to lose first one parent and then the other. She could understand his frustration and his anger, even his fear. But she couldn't understand and wouldn't tolerate any negativity. She'd chosen an aggressive course of treatment to deal with her cancer because she'd wanted to get on with her life, and if they were to have any kind of relationship, he had to understand that she wasn't a victim—she was a survivor.

She finished her glass of wine and stepped out of the tub, reaching for a towel. As she scrubbed it briskly over her body, she watched the bubbles drain away. When she realized what she was doing, she forced herself to pivot around, to face the mirror she'd automatically turned away from.

She'd been angry with Mason for not wanting to look at her, accused him of being afraid of what he might see. But the truth was, she hadn't really looked either. Not since the day the bandages had been removed after her surgery, almost two years earlier, had she dared to look at herself in a mirror. Then, she'd been so distressed by the raw red lines and dark slashing threads, she'd bawled like a baby. She'd thought she had been prepared for what it would look like—but all she could think was that it wasn't her breast, it didn't look anything like her. And in that moment, she'd regretted even having the reconstruction.

Dr. Allison had tried to talk to her about it, had assured her the swelling would go down, the scar would fade, but Zoe didn't care. She never intended for anyone to see her naked again.

In retrospect, she could admit it was unrealistic for a woman not even thirty—and not in a convent—to remain celibate for the rest of her life. But she'd been adamant at the time, determined to punish her body for its betrayal.

Later, of course, she'd been grateful for the reconstruction. Grateful she'd been able to present herself, at least to the outside world, like a whole normal woman. Now, however, she was preparing to face a man without the barriers of clothing or pretenses—to show him the woman she was, flaws and all, and ask him to accept her that way. But first, she had to accept herself.

So she drew in a deep breath and let the towel drop to the floor. Slowly her eyes tracked downward, and her breath released on a sigh. Dr. Allison had been right— the ugly red slash she remembered had faded so that it was now only a faint pink line.

As she looked at herself in the mirror, she realized that her reconstructed breast was a symbol of the woman she was—imperfect, but alive and healthy and determined to live her life to the fullest.

Mason's life hadn't changed in the four days that Zoe was gone. He had mostly kept to his usual routine— taking Rosie for walks every morning and night. If he'd lingered in front of Zoe's empty house on occasion, he was just being neighborly—keeping an eye on things while he knew she was away. But the heaviness in his heart had warned that it was more than that, and the ache of longing worried him.

Rosie had missed her, too. The animal would sit and stare longingly at the house, whimper forlornly, then look to Mason as if he blamed his master for Zoe's absence.

Mason suspected that he was to blame, that she wouldn't have accepted her ex-husband's offer to go the Caribbean if he hadn't screwed things up so completely. And the thought of her in the Caribbean with her ex-husband nearly drove him insane.

Although Zoe hadn't seemed to think Scott wanted anything more from her than the taking of some photographs, Mason hadn't been so sure. He'd tried to console himself with the fact that they were divorced, tried to assure himself that she would never have gotten involved with him on any level if she wasn't well and truly over her ex. But he'd known Zoe only three months and she'd been married to Scott for nine years, and she'd gone off to Exuma not just with her ex-husband but obviously ticked off at Mason. It was enough to make him wonder…and worry. Had he blown his chance with her completely? Would she come back?

It was on the third day of her absence that he'd finally acknowledged the truth that had been nudging at his subconscious for weeks—he'd fallen in love with her. He wasn't sure when or how it had happened, but he no longer doubted the depth of what he was feeling.

And he finally recognized the opportunity he'd been given when she walked into his life. Or maybe it was more accurate to say that he'd walked into hers. In any case, he knew it was an opportunity that he'd nearly squandered. He wouldn't make the same mistake again—not if he was given a second chance.

He'd paced a lot in the four days that she was gone, and tossed and turned in his bed. The house had seemed too silent somehow, too empty. The quiet had never bothered him before, the isolation had never worried him. He'd enjoyed his solitary existence, appreciated the freedom of doing what he wanted when he wanted.

Throughout his entire adult life, he'd been careful to keep his relationships with women simple, casual, easy. If the thought of falling in love had scared him, the idea of committing to one woman had terrified him. But that was before Zoe, before he'd realized that love could be a gift instead of a curse. Before he'd understood that an even scarier prospect than spending the rest of his life with one person was the possibility of spending the rest of his life without Zoe.

Yeah, she was only gone four days. But in those four days, he'd missed her. He'd missed her energy, her smile, the light that seemed to shine from within her. And he realized that he wanted her with him, every day, for the rest of his life.

Now, he only had to find a way to convince her to take a chance on him. Dinner, he hoped, would be the first step.

He'd never cooked for a woman before. Not anything more complicated than tossing some meat onto a barbecue, which he didn't figure really counted since he did the same thing whenever he had his buddies over for a meal. It wasn't that he couldn't cook, just that he'd never dated a woman for whom he wanted to make the effort. Until Zoe.

So many things had changed since she'd moved in next door. It was as if he could divide his life into two parts: "Before Zoe" and "After Zoe"—or, if he was lucky, "With Zoe."

He heard her moving around upstairs—getting dressed—and forced his thoughts away from *that* mental image to concentrate on dishing up the chicken and rice.

He was carrying the plates into the dining room when she came down the stairs. She was wearing a dress—it was short, sleeveless and scooped low in the front and the back. Her hair tumbled loose over her shoulders, the way he liked it best, and her skin was lightly tanned and glowing from the bath.

"I thought, since you went to so much trouble for dinner, I should dress up for the occasion."

"You looked great before. Now you look...a hell of a lot more tempting than dinner."

Her lips curved. "Dinner looks good to me."

It was only when she looked at the plates in his hand that he realized he was still holding them. He set them on the table, then held out her chair.

He kept the conversation casual during the meal. He could tell she was a little apprehensive, though he wasn't sure if her nerves were because she didn't know why he was there or because she did. He was experiencing some tension, too, because tonight he would either get everything he wanted—or lose the woman he loved.

"I was thinking about another alteration to the house plans," she said, after she'd finally pushed away her plate.

"You want to make changes now—when the renovations are almost finished?"

"Not a big change," she assured him.

"The client never thinks it's a big change."

She smiled, and the light in her eyes took his breath away. "I want a darkroom."

"A darkroom, huh? I seem to recall that we had a similar conversation once before and you claimed you didn't need one."

"I changed my mind."

"I'm glad."

"You are?"

"Yeah, because it means your trip was obviously a success."

"So much so that Scott offered me a job back at the magazine."

"And?" He didn't think she would need a darkroom

in her house in Pinehurst if she was planning to go back to New York City, but he wanted to be sure.

"And I turned him down. I don't want to be a fashion photographer anymore, but I've realized that I am still a photographer. That I still want to take pictures. Which means, of course, that I'll need somewhere to develop those pictures."

"I think we can work out something."

"Good." She smiled again.

He pushed away from the table, cleared their plates. Zoe followed him to the kitchen carrying the wineglasses and the half-empty bottle. They worked together loading the dishwasher and straightening the kitchen.

"Now are you going to tell me why you're really here?" she asked as she topped up their wineglasses.

"Because you told me to let you know when I figured out what I wanted...and I want you."

Her hand shook, splashing wine over the rim of the glass. She set the bottle down on the counter and concentrated on wiping up the spill with a towel. When she was finished, she folded the towel, hung it over the handle of the oven door, then—finally—faced him.

He laid his hands on her shoulders, then stroked them down her arms to her hands and linked their fingers together. "Now the question is—what do *you* want?"

"You," she admitted. "I think I've wanted you from the beginning. And when I came home and found you here, I started to hope, but I was afraid to hope and..."

The rest of the words faded away when he touched his lips to hers. Once, softly, briefly.

"I figured out something else, too," he told her.

"What's that?"

"That I love you."

He heard her soft intake of breath, saw the flicker of surprise, then wariness filled her deep brown eyes.

"Mason," she began.

"Shh." He brushed his mouth against hers again, silencing whatever she intended to say. "Don't say anything. Don't doubt it. Let me show you."

She couldn't refuse him something that she, too, wanted. Instead, she took his hand and led him up the stairs to her bedroom.

Her heart was pounding, her blood was pumping, and her stomach was a tangled knot of nerves and anticipation. She wanted this—it seemed as if she'd wanted this forever. But she was also terrified that despite the reassurance of his words, the tenderness of his touch and the passion in his kiss, he would decide she wasn't what he wanted after all.

He stroked a hand gently over her hair. "You're trembling."

"I'm scared," she admitted softly.

"Am I moving too fast? I don't want—"

"No. You're not moving too fast. I'm just worried that you'll be disappointed."

"Never," he promised. "Although I have to admit that I'm a little scared, too."

"What are you afraid of?"

"Touching you—or not touching you." His mouth curved in a wry smile. "Does that make any sense?"

She nodded, understanding completely. "So much for sex being simple, huh?"

"Sex *is* simple. What's between us is more than sex."

"It doesn't have to be. We don't have to complicate this."

"It's already complicated," he told her. "But I'm finding I don't mind that as much as I thought I would."

Then he kissed her again. And the touch of his mouth to hers, that slow, sensual glide of his lips, wiped her mind of everything except the here and now. As the kiss deepened, her desire escalated and the last vestiges of fear faded away.

His touch was as patient and unhurried as his kiss, his hands trailing down her back, slowly stroking up again. When he tugged down the zipper at the back of her dress, she didn't try to stop him. When he pushed the straps over her shoulders, she let the garment slither down to the floor, leaving her clad in only a lacy pink bra and matching bikini panties.

He lowered his head and kissed the curve of her breasts above the scalloped edge of her bra, first one breast, then the other. Then his tongue dipped into the valley between them, and she shuddered.

He scooped her off the floor and carried her to the bed, laying her down gently on the covers. She pulled him down with her and fused her mouth to his. Their kiss was hot and hungry now, as greedy and impatient as the hands that dragged at his shirt, seeking and finding hard, bare skin. Her palms slid over his belly, his chest, his shoulders, stroking the smooth, sleek muscles.

He drew away to yank the shirt over his head, toss it aside. She found the button at the front of his pants, urging him to discard those as well and revealing a pair of dark, sexy boxer briefs. Then he was kissing her again, his hands were on her again, and the glorious weight of his body was pressing hers into the mattress. She wrapped her arms around him, locked her legs around his, and gave herself over to the passion he'd reawakened.

He found the center clasp of her bra and with a quick flick, it was open. She stilled. It was an automatic response, an instinctive reaction, and one that she cursed herself for even knowing she couldn't prevent it.

But he didn't miss a beat. And as his hands and his lips continued their exquisite torture, she found herself relaxing again.

His mouth skimmed down her throat, lower. His hands were on her breasts, then sliding over her hips, down her thighs. His lips were on her breasts, first one, then the other. He lingered a moment at her nipple—and though she couldn't really feel anything there, she didn't dissuade him. He was clearly enjoying his exploration of her body, and the realization was exhilarating. Then he moved over to the other nipple, his tongue circling the base, his lips closing over the turgid peak.

"You are beautiful, Zoe. And perfect just the way you are."

She shook her head, but he ignored her wordless protest. His hands and his mouth continued their leisurely sensual exploration, exploring all of the dips and curves of her body with such devastating thoroughness she was breathless and quivering with wanting.

"Mason, please."

His hands skimmed down the outside of her thighs, then up the inside. "I'm not going to be rushed," he said. "Not this time."

It was exquisite torture, the slow, steady building of heat and tension deep inside. His knee slid between hers, nudging apart her thighs, and she thought, *finally*.

But still he didn't hurry. Still he teased and tormented until her nerves were stretched so taut she thought they might snap. His fingertips skated up the inside of her thigh, then down again. Each time, moving just a little higher, a little closer to where she was practically begging to be touched. When his thumb brushed over the moist curls at the apex of her thighs, she gasped. When it started to move in slow, gentle circles over the nub at her center, she actually whimpered. When he slid his finger between the slick folds and into her, she flew apart.

She barely had a chance to catch her breath before he was driving her up again. Only then did he finally sheath himself with a condom and rise over her.

In one smooth stroke, he slid into her—not just filling her, but fulfilling her. She let her eyes drift shut as she lost herself in the erotic pleasure of his body inside her. Their bodies moved together in perfect rhythm, as if they'd joined like this a thousand times instead of only once before. It was, in so many ways, like a homecoming.

"Look at me, Zoe."

She opened her eyes, found his fixed on her. The emotion in his gaze took her breath away.

"I want you to see that I'm looking at you," he

said. "I want you to know that I want only you—for now and forever."

Then he kissed her again.

As his lips moved over hers, his body moved inside of hers, she felt the tension building inside again.

His arms came around her, anchoring her, as she shuddered and sobbed through the waves of release that battered her into mindless, boneless submission, then finally dragged him under with her.

She was exhausted.

Wonderfully, fabulously, gloriously exhausted. And though she was pinned to the mattress beneath the weight of Mason's inert body, she didn't mind. In fact, she was a little disappointed when he finally lifted himself off her, landing face-first on the pillow. But then he shifted to his side and tucked her against him, holding her close.

"Remember what I said about taking things slow?" he asked.

She nodded against his shoulder.

"Well, I don't want to take it slow anymore."

"Since we're naked in my bed, I'd say that's a good thing."

"I wasn't just talking about making love with you— although I'm definitely glad we've moved ahead in that direction."

"Then what were you talking about?"

His hand stroked down her side, from her shoulder to her hip in a lazy caress that both soothed and aroused. "Building a future together."

"I thought we would just take things one day at a time."

"I want to marry you, Zoe."

She froze as both euphoria and terror filled her heart.

"Aren't you going to say something?" he asked after a long moment of silence.

Her head was spinning so that she couldn't think, never mind talk. I. Want. To. Marry. You. She sucked in a deep breath, blew it out again. "Why?"

He propped himself up on an elbow to look at her. "Because I love you and I want to share my life with you."

"You don't—you can't—"

He silenced her with a kiss. "I can and I do."

She shook her head. "It's too much, too soon."

"Is it?" His tone was deliberately casual. "Are there rules about this sort of thing?"

"You know what I mean."

"Actually, I don't. I've never been in love before, so I'm not familiar with the procedure or protocol. But I do know what I'm feeling, and everything just feels right when I'm with you.

"I've spent my entire adult life avoiding any kind of serious relationships without even realizing it. Tyler told me that any first-year psych student could figure out why—because the loss of first my mother then my father made me put shields up around my heart so it wouldn't ever take that kind of emotional hit again.

"Maybe there's some truth to that," he allowed. "Or maybe it's even simpler—maybe I just never found anyone that I wanted to get serious with. Until you."

He cradled her face in his hands, gently tipped her

head back so that she had no choice but to meet his gaze. "I love you, Zoe."

Her eyes filled with tears. "Damn you, Mason."

"That's not quite the reaction I was expecting."

"Well, I never expected to hear you say those three words."

"I've never said them before," he told her. "To anyone."

The tears spilled over. "You shouldn't have said them now—not to me."

He kissed away the tears, brushing his lips over the wet trail on one cheek, then the other, in a gesture so tender it caused more tears to spill over.

"Why not?" he asked gently.

She swallowed. "Because I already screwed up one marriage—the last thing I want is to jump into another."

"Do you love me, Zoe?"

"I don't think I could be here with you now if I didn't."

This time when he kissed her, it was harder, fiercer and somehow triumphant. "Then marry me," he said. "So that we can start building our life together."

She didn't know what to say, how to respond to the man who was offering her everything she'd wanted for so long. She was tempted and she was terrified, and, most of all, she was worried that regardless of whether she said "yes" or "no," she would somehow end up hurting him.

"What do you say, Zoe?"

He was the man who'd loved her with frenzied passion and exquisite tenderness, who'd touched not just her body but her heart and healed the wounds that went so much deeper than the physical scars on her body. The man she loved.

Though she couldn't deny her feelings for him, she had no intention of making a life-altering decision after knowing him only three months. It was ridiculous to even consider anything different.

But when she opened her mouth to tell him just that, she heard herself saying "yes" instead.

Chapter Thirteen

Zoe held out her hand.

Her friend stared, speechless, at the diamonds winking from her third finger. "You're getting married?"

"Tell me I'm not crazy."

"You're definitely crazy," Claire said, then grinned. "But I'm so happy for you."

"You don't think it's too soon?"

"Time doesn't have anything to do with it," her friend said. "The only thing that matters is how you feel about each other."

"I've only known him three months, but I already can't imagine my life without him," Zoe admitted. "He makes me feel—I can't even describe how I feel when

I'm with him. Except that I've never felt like this before. I feel happy and hopeful, as if our future together can be anything we want it to be."

"That's exactly how you should feel when you're starting a life with the person you love."

"I do love him," she said. "I thought, after my marriage to Scott fell apart, that I would never be able to love someone again. I know I didn't want to. But suddenly Mason was just there, in my heart, filling it full of feelings I didn't ever expect to have again."

"You deserve this," Claire said, hugging her tight. "Have you set a date yet?"

"October sixth."

"Not this October?"

Zoe nodded. "I know it's quick. But Mason said he doesn't want to wait any longer than absolutely necessary to start our life together. I told him I couldn't plan a wedding in less than four months—so we compromised on two."

"If you need any help, let me know," Claire said. "I'd love to—"

"Be my matron of honor?"

Claire stared at her. "Are you serious?"

Zoe nodded.

"But you must have friends you've known longer than me—"

"No one who knows me better," she interrupted. "Certainly no one who's been there for me the way you've been. And no one who means as much to me as you do."

Her friends soft grey eyes shimmered with moisture. "Okay then," she sniffled and blinked back the tears.

"Two months isn't very much time, we better start making plans."

"It's going to be a small wedding," Zoe said. "Probably outside at Hadfield House, if the weather's good."

"We can get a tent to have the reception there, too." Claire pulled open a drawer where she found a pad of paper and a pen to take notes. "I know a great caterer. Did you want a sit-down meal or just hors d'oeuvres? A band or a D.J.? Real flowers or silk?"

Zoe's head was spinning. Mason had proposed only the night before, and put the ring on her finger that morning. She hadn't had a chance to think about any of the details yet—or to panic about everything that needed to be done in such a short time.

Suddenly Claire looked up from the paper, her eyes wide as another thought occurred. "And who's going to take the pictures?"

Over the next six weeks, Zoe and Claire worked out all of the details. As the day of the wedding drew nearer, Zoe found herself really looking forward to the occasion—and especially to starting her life with Mason.

Until the morning, less than two weeks before their scheduled exchange of vows, that she found the lump.

Mason had left early for work—although he'd taken time to make love with her before rushing off to a job site—and she'd reluctantly forced herself out of the comfort of her bed to shower and start her own day.

She was rubbing shower gel over her skin and thinking that she should schedule a pedicure before the wedding when she felt something on the underside of her breast.

Despite the steam rising from the water, she felt an immediate chill—an icy-cold that encapsulated her whole body. Suddenly weak in the knees, she braced her forearms on the tile, leaned her head against them, and forced herself to breathe.

"It's not a lump." She spoke aloud, as if hearing the echo of the words might convince her that they were true. "Of course it's not a lump. The breast is gone—I'm just being paranoid, afraid to let myself be happy."

But her fingers moved automatically to the underside of her breast, hesitating just below where she'd felt the ridge. "There's nothing there," she said to herself, and slid her fingertips over the skin.

But it wasn't nothing. It was something—a definite thickening of tissue between the implant and the wall of her chest.

"It's not cancer."

She repeated those words over and over again, reminding herself that there were numerous other possible explanations for the strange bump under her skin. It could be a cyst or a fibroadenoma. And even if it was a tumor, it could be benign.

But even as she considered the various possibilities, the one that remained at the forefront of her mind was cancer.

She knew that there was a ten percent risk of a local recurrence after surgery, and that ninety percent of such recurrences happened within the first five years of the surgery. She also knew that better than eighty percent of women with an isolated local recurrence following mastectomy eventually developed distant metastases.

And even with all of the research being done, that was always a grim prognosis.

Yeah, she knew all of the numbers, all of the cold, hard facts, and they terrified her.

She sank to her knees in the shower, buried her face in her hands and sobbed until the water turned cold.

As Mason headed back to Zoe's after work on Monday, he couldn't shake the feeling that something was wrong with Zoe. For a few days now, she'd been quiet and withdrawn and he didn't have the slightest idea why. She'd been busy over the past couple of months, making plans for the wedding and final preparations for the bed-and-breakfast, which she would open to guests in the spring, but she hadn't seemed overly stressed or preoccupied with anything.

Not until Friday, he decided, thinking back. She'd been fine in the morning when he'd said good-bye, but definitely distracted when he got home. He wondered if her preoccupation had anything to do with the call he'd received earlier that day, and when he got home, he asked her about it.

"The caterer contacted me today," he said. "He said you haven't got back to him with the final numbers for the reception."

"Actually, I wanted to talk to you about that."

"The numbers?"

"The wedding." She took the tray of manicotti out of the oven, lifted the foil to check it. "I think we should postpone the wedding."

"What?"

"It's just too soon. Everything's happening too fast."

He stared at her—at the back of her head, actually, since she seemed more interested in the pasta than in discussing their wedding.

He strode over to the oven, pushed the foil back down on the tray and forced her to look at him. "We set the date two months ago—"

"I was obviously out of my mind to agree to plan a wedding in two months."

"Not only did you agree to do it," he pointed out, "You've done it. Everything is ready for our wedding in nine days, so why would you want to postpone it now?"

"It just seems like we're rushing into this," she said.

"I thought we agreed there wasn't any reason to wait."

She glanced away. "I think a spring wedding would be nice."

"What's wrong with a fall wedding?"

"I got married in the fall the first time and—"

"You got married in January."

She frowned.

"Obviously you don't remember telling me that."

"My point is that it would be nicer to get married in the garden when the flowers are blooming."

His eyes narrowed. "What's going on, Zoe?"

"I just think we should wait a few months."

"Why?"

"Please." Her eyes were suspiciously bright. "I just need some more time."

His heart sank. "I love you, Zoe."

She didn't say the words back. In fact, she didn't say anything at all, and her silence was like a knife through his heart.

From the moment he'd realized he'd fallen in love with Zoe, he'd been certain about what he wanted. He'd been so certain, in fact, that it hadn't occurred to him she might not want the same thing. He hadn't considered that she might have reservations about getting married. Sure, she'd been hesitant when he'd first proposed, but he'd assumed her reluctance had been simply because she'd been so recently divorced. He hadn't worried that he'd pushed her too far too fast, that she might not love him as completely and wholeheartedly as he loved her.

And considering that possibility now was almost more than he could stand, but he had to know. "Do you love me, Zoe?"

She didn't meet his gaze. "I need time to be sure about my feelings."

Zoe hadn't expected that he would come back, certainly not that same night. And she hadn't expected that when he did come back, it would be with steely determination in his eyes.

"No," he said.

"What?"

"We're not postponing the wedding."

She folded her arms over her chest. "You don't get to make that decision unilaterally."

"We set the date together," he reminded her.

"Fine—let's change it together."

"No."

"You're being unreasonable."

His only response was to haul her into his arms and kiss her. She tasted his fury and frustration and, beneath the surface of those emotions, hurt and need.

She tried to resist—she really did. She knew what he was doing, trying to make her respond to his touch, to prove her feelings for him. But even knowing it, she couldn't prevent it. She couldn't deny the way her lips softened beneath his or the way her body yielded to his anymore than she could hold back the silent tears that spilled onto her cheeks as she kissed him back.

His lips softened and his hands lifted to cradle her face, his thumbs gently brushing the tears away. "Tell me you don't love me."

"I don't love you."

But the tears were streaming now, the anguish in her eyes undeniable.

"Now tell me why," he said.

And finally she did. She told him about finding the lump in the shower and her appointment earlier that day with Dr. Allison, who had tried to be reassuring but had done a core needle biopsy to determine the exact nature of the problem.

He held her while she cried, and he cried right along with her. But he never turned away from her, he never tried to downplay her concerns or her emotions. He did give her hell for not telling him right away—and for not letting him go with her to the appointment—but mostly he was just there for her as no one but Claire had ever been before.

"When will your doctor have the results?"

"I have a three o'clock appointment on Thursday."

"I'm taking you."

"You don't have—"

"I love you, Zoe."

He said it softly but with such conviction, she couldn't deny him the expression of her own feelings. She took his hand and led him upstairs to the bedroom. And she told him not just in words, but with her body and her heart, how much she loved him. She loved him with everything she had, everything she was, as if it might be their last time together.

Claire was the first person Zoe had told about finding the irregularity in her breast—the only person, in fact, until Mason had managed to pry the information out of her. And she was the one person who was with Zoe when she got the phone call early Wednesday morning changing her scheduled appointment with Dr. Allison.

"Are you going to let your fiancé know about the new appointment?" Claire asked when Zoe got off the phone.

"No, because then he'll juggle his schedule to try to go with me, and it really isn't necessary."

"I know you're worried," Claire said gently. "You don't have to pretend you're not."

"Of course, I'm worried, but I'll handle it. I'm not so sure Mason can."

"How do you think he'll handle it if he finds out you went without him?"

"That's really not on the top of my list of concerns right now."

"Is the wedding on that list?" Claire wanted to know. "Because you're supposed to be getting married in three days."

Zoe sighed as she zipped up her overnight bag—she wasn't planning on staying in the city but, not knowing the results of her biopsy, thought it was best to be prepared.

"He loves you," Claire said gently.

She nodded. Over the past few weeks, Mason had proven that to her in more ways than she could count. Even when she'd finally told him about the lump, he'd stood firm, insisting that he loved her and wanted to marry her. And although Zoe loved him even more for his conviction, too much had changed since his original proposal for her to hold him to it.

"Enough to stand by you no matter what happens," her friend continued.

Zoe knew that was probably true. But she loved him too much to put him through the hell of a second diagnosis and everything that might entail.

She closed her eyes, her grip instinctively tightening on the handle of her bag. God, she didn't even want to think about what would come after. Since she'd found the suspicious thickening on the underside of her reconstructed breast—she was terrified to even call it a lump—she'd been concentrating only on the first step: get to the doctor. She hadn't wanted to think any further than that, had been terrified by the possibilities.

"Let me come with you," Claire said.

"You have your book club tonight, and I'm not sure what time I'll get back or if I'll have to stay."

"I can skip my book club for one week."

Zoe shook her head.

Claire sighed and excused herself to boil the kettle while Zoe threw some things in an overnight bag. When Claire returned with two cups of peppermint tea, she studied her friend closely.

Zoe sensed her scrutiny, and the question she hesitated to ask. But when she finished her tea and set the cup aside to pick up her bag, Claire finally said, "Are you coming back?"

She forced a smile. "I only packed two pairs of underwear."

"Then I'll expect to see you on Friday."

Claire folded her friend in her arms and hugged her tightly; Zoe's throat was constricted as she returned the embrace.

She didn't look back as she made her way down the stairs. If she did, she might break down, and she couldn't get through this if she broke down.

One step at a time, she reminded herself, reaching for the handle of the door.

She blinked against the brightness of the sunshine as she stepped out onto the porch—and came face-to-face with Mason.

Zoe blinked again, thinking that he might be just an illusion, but when she opened her eyes, he was still there.

And pissed off, if his narrowed gaze and set jaw were any indication.

Her heart bumped hard against her ribs.

She didn't have to ask how he'd known. No doubt Claire had called him when she'd gone downstairs to make the tea. And though Zoe wanted to be angry with her friend, she knew her actions had been motivated by love and concern for her.

Mason pried her fingers from the handle of her bag, then slung it over his shoulder.

"Let's go," he said tersely.

She wanted to refuse, to dig in her heels, but he was already tossing her bag into the back of the MDX.

He opened the passenger door, and waited. Despite his silence, she sensed his impatience, as obvious as the anger that showed in the stiffness of his posture and the flex of the muscle in his jaw.

"Mason—"

"Just get in the car."

She flinched at the fury in his tone, started toward the open door, then stopped. "You know, I didn't ask you to go with me and—"

"No, you didn't, did you?" he interrupted. "In fact, you didn't even tell me you had an appointment today."

And that was when she realized he wasn't just angry, he was hurt. She felt a pang of regret that she'd caused him pain—the last thing she'd wanted to do was hurt him. But she knew he would be hurt a lot more if the results of her biopsy weren't good.

"I thought it would be better if I handled this on my own," she said softly.

"You're wearing my ring on your finger," he reminded her. "That means you don't handle anything on your own."

She touched his arm. "I know how hard this is for you."

"I don't think you do."

"That's why I wanted to deal with this on my own."

He shook his head. "Do you know what's the worst thing about this whole situation? It's not that you're facing the possibility of another battle with cancer, because you've done that once already and proven that you can win. It's that you don't trust me enough to stick by you if you have to do it again."

"That's not true," she denied.

He stared at her hard. "Isn't it?"

And she realized that maybe he was right. Maybe she hadn't wanted to tell him about the appointment because she didn't trust that he would be there for her as she needed him to be there for her, and if she didn't have any expectations, she wouldn't be disappointed.

"I'm not your ex-husband," he said gently.

"I know," she said, and in that moment, she finally accepted that it was true. "I'm sorry."

"I don't want an apology, I want your trust. But obviously we need to work on that some more." He waited until she was in the SUV, then he closed the door and went around to the driver's side.

"Where are you going?" she asked, when he turned toward downtown instead of the highway.

"To the courthouse."

"Why?"

"To pick up our marriage license."

She didn't say anything. The last thing she wanted was to get into a discussion about their wedding when she still wasn't even sure if it would happen.

You're supposed to be getting married in three days.

Claire's statement echoed in her mind, as did the question implicit in it.

I'm not your ex-husband.

No, he wasn't. And he would stand by her. She didn't doubt that any longer. But it would break his heart to do so, and she couldn't do that to him.

He pulled into the parking lot of the courthouse.

"Come on," he said.

She didn't think they both needed to be there to pick up a piece of paper, but she got out of the vehicle anyway.

There was nothing she wanted more than to marry Mason and live happily-ever-after with him, but the harsh reality was that her visit to Dr. Allison today could bring her whole castle in the clouds tumbling down around her. She wanted to think positively. She was trying really hard to retain an optimistic outlook, but the doubts and fears kept crowding in.

"Couldn't we pick up our marriage license on the way back?" she finally asked.

"We probably could," he agreed. "But the JP could only squeeze us in this morning."

"Why do we need to see the JP?"

"To get married."

His words stopped her dead in her tracks. "You can't be serious."

He turned to face her. "Why not?"

"Because we have a wedding planned for Saturday afternoon—"

"A wedding that you have no intention of showing up for if the news you get from Dr. Allison isn't what you want to hear."

She couldn't deny it, so she said, "This is ridiculous. We have almost fifty people—"

"I don't give a damn about our guests or the cake or the caterer or any one of the thousand other details that I'm sure went into planning the event, and I don't believe you really do, either. The only thing that matters is the vows—the pledging of our hearts to one another, the promise to stick together no matter what the future might bring."

He sounded as if he really meant it, and when he kissed her, she knew that he did. She hadn't realized that she was crying until he kissed her tears away, his lips brushing over first one cheek, then the other.

"I've cried more in the past week than in the past ten years," she told him. "And it's usually on your shoulder."

"I'm not afraid of a few tears."

"It could get a lot worse before it gets better."

"I know—but we'll focus on the 'better' part. Whatever happens, we'll be together. We'll face the future together."

Two hours later, Zoe was standing in the back of an elevator, twisting her brand-new wedding band on her finger. She still wondered if she should have been stronger, somehow found the strength to hold firm in her conviction to wait. But it was done now—they were officially married. And though she still worried about their future, she was relieved to know that she didn't have to be strong all by herself anymore. Whatever happened, he would be there for her, as she would be there for him.

When the bell dinged to announce their arrival on the

sixteenth floor, Mason touched his hand to the small of her back, gently propelling her forward.

She moved ahead, because his strength gave her strength. If he was strong enough to face this with her, she would be strong enough, too.

She glanced up at him, saw that his jaw was set, his eyes hard and focused, and the pulse in his throat was racing. She loved him so much, but never more so than in that very moment, and she took his hand, linking their fingers together as much for reassurance as to reassure.

He paused outside the door with Dr. Allison's name on it.

"I love you," he said. "For now and for always."

She tried to smile, but her lips trembled rather than curved. She tried to speak, to tell him that she loved him, too, but her throat was too tight to allow the words to escape.

"I know," he said softly to her, and managed a smile. "You don't have to say anything, because I know. And that's all that matters."

And Zoe knew that no matter what Dr. Allison had to tell her today, she could handle it with Mason by her side.

Epilogue

Rain was pounding on the roof when Zoe woke up.

She snuggled deeper under the covers, and sighed contentedly when she felt Mason's arm curl around her before he tugged her back against the warmth of his body.

"It's raining," she told him.

"Just like the day we got married," her husband noted.

He wasn't talking about the day of their courthouse ceremony but the day they'd renewed their vows in front of their family—including her mother, who had come from Montana with potential husband number five, and his eighty-one-year-old grandmother and her husband, who had made the trip from Florida in their RV—and friends. The weather had been gray and drizzly and dreary, but Zoe hadn't cared. Everything was right in her world because three days earlier, she'd found out that the lump she'd so feared was only scar tissue.

Now, three *years* later, Zoe and Mason were celebrating not just their third anniversary but her fifth year cancer-free.

"What are we going to do today?" she asked.

"Whatever you want, so long as it doesn't involve a visit to Hadfield House or a camera."

She smiled at that.

For the first two years of their marriage, they'd lived in Hadfield House, where she'd juggled her responsibilities as manager of the bed-and-breakfast with the demands of her newly launched business as a special occasion photographer. But both ventures had proven to be incredibly successful, forcing Zoe to make a choice. Six months ago, she'd hired another manager for Hadfield House, and she and Mason had moved out and into their new home—designed by Mason and built by his brother.

"I had thought I would be sad to leave Hadfield House," she admitted. "But it was time to move on."

"You'd accomplished what you needed to there," he agreed.

Something in his tone suggested that he understood more about the connection she felt to the house than she'd ever told him.

"What do you mean?"

"I'm not so clueless that I couldn't figure out that you needed to make something of that old house in order to heal yourself."

"I never would have said you were clueless," she assured him. "Although I never would have guessed you were that insightful, either."

"I'm proud of you, Zoe. And grateful, every day, that you are in my life."

He kissed her then, and she sighed her pleasure as her eyes drifted shut and her body melted against his.

"I have some ideas about how we can spend our anniversary," he murmured the words against her lips. "And they don't require leaving this room."

She wriggled closer to him. "Sounds interesting."

As his hands slipped beneath her pajama top, there was an impatient scratch at the door.

He groaned; she giggled.

"That beast is a menace," he said, echoing the statement she'd made to him so long ago.

But the words were no sooner out of his mouth than a cry came through the baby monitor. The sound of their ten-month-old son, adopted only three months earlier, filled her heart to overflowing with joy and pride and fear.

Mason was already out of bed and reaching for his jeans. "I'll take care of the dog, you take care of Liam."

She tied her robe around her waist and padded across the hall to the nursery, where their little boy was fussing.

"Good morning, my baby." She scooped him into her arms and held him close, breathing in his sweet baby scent.

Liam squawked and wriggled.

"I know—diaper, then breakfast, then cuddles," she said, laying him on the change table to take care of the first task.

She heard Rosie barking outside, and when Liam had a dry diaper on his bottom, she carried him to the window to watch the crazy dog dancing around in the rain.

"Da!" Liam clapped his hands together, a mile-wide smile lighting up his face.

"Yeah, there's your daddy."

"Ro!"

"And Rosie," she confirmed, then turned the baby around in her arms. "You know, you really need to learn how to say 'Mama.'"

He just stared at her with his big blue eyes.

"Bu-ba."

"Alright—we'll go get your bottle."

Mason came in, damp from the rain, just as she was settling Liam into his high chair with his juice.

"Hey, big guy." He dropped a kiss on the top of his son's head. "What are you and Mama making for breakfast today?"

"Ma!"

She nearly dropped the carton of eggs she'd taken out of the fridge. "What did he just say?"

"'Ma'—he says it all the time."

She put the eggs on the counter and turned around. "I've never heard him say it before."

He just shrugged. "It's usually when you're not here—when he's looking around for you and just before he starts screaming because he can't find you."

She smiled at that. "He looks for me?"

"Of course he looks for you—you're the center of his world." He wrapped his arms around her, nuzzled her throat. "Just as you're the center of mine."

Rosie barked.

"And his, too, apparently," Mason noted.

Zoe laughed and linked her hands behind his neck. "You know, I think I really like this life we've built together."

"I think I do, too," he said, and kissed her.

Somewhere in the background she registered the sound of the dog barking, the baby banging his bottle on the tray of his high chair and the telephone ringing.

"And though I sometimes wish it was a little less chaotic," he admitted, "it is ours."

And the best part, she knew, was that their life together had only just begun.

Cut from the soap opera that made her a star, America's
TV goddess Gloria Hart heads back to her childhood
home to regroup. But when a car crash maroons her in
small-town Mississippi, it's local housewife Jenny Miller
to the rescue. Soon these two very different women,
together with Gloria's sassy assistant, become fast friends,
realizing that they bring out a certain secret something
in each other that men find irresistible!

Look for

The Secret Goddess Code

by

PEGGY WEBB

Available November wherever you buy books.

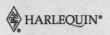

HARLEQUIN®

Mediterranean NIGHTS™

*Not everything is above board
on Alexandra's Dream!*

*Enjoy plenty of secrets, drama and sensuality
in the latest from Mediterranean Nights.*

Coming in November 2007...

BELOW DECK

by

Dorien Kelly

Determined to protect her young son,
widow Mei Lin Wang keeps him hidden
aboard *Alexandra's Dream* under cover of
her job. But life gets extremely complicated
when the ship's security officer, Gideon Dayan,
is piqued by the mystery surrounding this
beautiful, haunted woman....

ATHENA FORCE

Heart-pounding romance and thrilling adventure.

History repeats itself...unless she can stop it.

Investigative reporter Winter Archer is thrown into writing a biography of Athena Academy's founder. But someone out there will stop at nothing—not even murder—to ensure that long-buried secrets remain hidden.

ATHENA FORCE

Will the women of Athena unravel Arachne's powerful web of blackmail and death...or succumb to their enemies' deadly secrets?

Look for

VENDETTA
by *Meredith Fletcher*

Available November wherever you buy books.

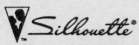